THIS GODFORSAKEN PLACE

THIS GODFORSAKEN PLACE

CINDA GAULT

BRINDLE
& GLASS

LIBRARY AND ARCHIVES CANADA CATALOGUING IN PUBLICATION
Gault, Cinda, author
This godforsaken place / Cinda Gault.

Issued in print and electronic formats.
ISBN 978-1-927366-41-7
I. Title.
PS8563.A84448T45 2015   C813'.54   C2014-908204-5

Cover image: *Winter Sunset with Horses*, Rike_, istockphoto.com
Grunge Clouds Background, kirstypargeter, istockphoto.com
Editor: Melva McLean
Cover design: Pete Kohut
Author photo: David Leyes

This book is a work of fiction based on some historical events. Names, characters, places, and incidents are either fictitious or used in a fictitiously.

Brindle & Glass Publishing acknowledges the financial support of the Canada Council for the Arts, the British Columbia Arts Council, and the Government of Canada through the Canada Book Fund (CBF). Brindle & Glass Publishing also acknowledges the financial support of the Province of British Columbia through the Book Publishing Tax Credit.

 Canadian Patrimoine Heritage canadien   Canada Council Conseil des Arts for the Arts du Canada   BRITISH COLUMBIA ARTS COUNCIL

PRINTED IN CANADA AT FRIESENS
15 16 17 18 19 5 4 3 2 1

To Gary, Gannon, and Dillon—my heroes

hea Wyatt has hounded me into writing this personal history, as though what happened a dozen years ago is of any use to anyone. I tell him crevices of time have always been packed with the unremarkable minutiae of ordinary lives, but ultimately it does not matter what oddities old Aunt Eunice doodled on her notebook or what kind of waistcoat Uncle Ramsay might have worn in a particular century. Patterns of ancient wallpaper should rightfully fade to blank. Remarkably resistant to sensible argument, Wyatt will not let me dislodge from his mind the conviction that there is value in documenting what, in my opinion, is just as well left alone.

In any case, I have spent hours that I will never be able to recoup in the recalling of what I have mostly forgotten. When I protest there is no need to tout personal business from the rooftops, he counters (with some pomposity) that future generations who might see this story as relevant to their self-understanding are entitled to know the facts. This view is just another permutation of the sense of history I was fed: one cannot understand the present day without knowing and honouring the past.

Hogwash.

We pick and choose our past just as surely as we pick and choose our future. I do not like this business of thinking ourselves determined by larger forces, be they divine or otherwise. What will be forgotten, remembered, dwelt upon, and minimized is a matter of choice. Shall we choose to remember our mistakes or our successes? The injustices we have meted out or those done against us? Will we condemn our children to a world apparently inherited from bumpkins and evildoers lurching from one ill-conceived idea to the next? The occurrence of an event does not mean we should immortalize it or keep going back to it as a dog to vomit. Under the weight of history, dreams thrash about until they tire and sink rather than find sturdy footholds of strength and confidence. Despite all platitudes to the contrary, principled living requires values, not a benighted past.

Wyatt insists on history. I know well enough that once he sets his mind on something he will not stop talking about it. Since I can stomach only so much jabber, I have resigned myself. To my mind, Posterity, you might better occupy yourself with the drama of your own lives. In the end, we all have to confront the reality that stands before us.

—Abigail Peacock

TRAPPED

No matter how much I wanted to deny it, I had to admit that I was inescapably trapped, bayed in this godforsaken place, and brought to my knees with the despair of it.

Pitiful. I'll try again.

I was hardly able to remember the time two years earlier when Father and I, still snug in the bosom of dear England, heard in the word *Canada* the very timbre of adventure.

Better. Sufficiently distant and superficial to offer at least some resistance to the maudlin.

From three thousand miles away, this rugged land promised a vast wilderness of exotic men and beasts. Our cramped imaginations reeled at the enormity and natural majesty of this place.

Entirely disingenuous. How stupid and naïve we were, sailing all this way only to stall out in an ocean of scrub trees where every day demoralized. In summer, wild creatures stalked through the bush like their predator shark cousins once trailed slave ships. From the sky, black flies, horseflies, and mosquitoes—the Devil's own vanguard— struck with poisoned spears, inflicting eye-streaming malevolence. Even when hope presented itself in an outcropping of rock or expanse of lake, uplifting breezes inevitably ran aground in tangled bush with no defining shores.

Worse, autumn temperatures crashed into an instant ice age, so dramatic a departure from England's dependable mists as to fuel suspicion of any inclination toward the extreme. Overnight brought a new avalanche of dangers: hypothermia, starvation, isolation, and a pervading, bone-chilling dryness. Something so ostensibly uncompli- cated as an evening walk meant risking frostbite to stumble along the frozen wagon ruts called Main Street. Every town on this continent had a Main Street, the numbing poetic consequence of hewing and drawing.

If that was not enough, ragtag people from all over the globe came here hoping a fresh start would make up for a lifetime of bad luck or wrong-headed decisions. Father and I were just as bad. We had no idea our grand adventure would imprison us in a ten-by-twelve-foot shanty. After he fell ill, and for the first time could not drag himself out of bed, I did not know what to do.

Days bled into each other until I considered it a victory that I even knew the month and year I was alive. I had to admit a measure of sheepishness in having lost any semblance whatsoever of a backbone, and so filled my sails with the miners' optimism that gold might soon be found. On each new tack, I rehearsed that a gold strike would attract new prospectors and their women and children. We might one day build a proper community and together generate a life worth living.

What I could not allow to overtake me was my real and over- whelming conviction that this place would never be anything but what it was, and I was joined at the hip with it.

How I wished for some warm-hearted friend, a receptive ear that might provide some reassurance that my trials on this earth mattered to someone. And yet, as comforting as the outpouring of my heart would have been, I was unable to shake the sense of danger inherent in expressing fear at all. Was I tempting disaster by admitting weakness? I could only too vividly predict Father's reaction to my anguish. His devastation would run straight to self-recrimination because he was the one who suggested coming here in the first place. If my fellow pioneers knew my opinions of this blight on the map they already called home, I suspected they would recoil from their friendly nods and idle chitchat. How could they not, considering how harshly I judged all life choices that led to here?

This place was not what I expected at all. It robbed all nuance—the water either did or did not freeze, the fire did or did not ignite, the door would or would not open when the snow piled high. Every hut and shed in this village was only marginally sturdier than a lean-to. If you made the mistake of spilling water at Christmas, you had to live with it as a slick of ice on your floorboards until spring, since the wood stove heated no more than the distance of warming hands. Warmth wept into usurping cold, draining the will to go on.

My fears flapped in a desperate search for some crack in my prison, a hairline of daylight they might worry open into a possible escape route. Eventually they exhausted themselves, forcing me once again to conclude there was nothing I could do about my present crisis. Sometimes, when I was sure Father was sleeping or unconscious in whatever anesthetized world he had created for himself, I consoled myself out loud that we were still better off than most. The men, new in town, had to live at Lars Larsen's, where they paid for the use of his bare wooden floor and the right to shiver along a well-worn path to the communal outhouse. He rented frozen sleeping space to prospectors who all had to squeeze into his tiny shack. At least Father had his own bed in which to gasp and hack. Repeating this aloud, even in a whisper, staved off panic, if only for a while.

The Swedes on Lars's floor trudged off each morning like Snow White's dwarfs, happy in their simple-minded search for treasure. I did not go down into their mine with them to see what they did, but at the end of their day, back they came, all smudged and rumpled, to work together like beavers on a new lodge. Lars had taken advantage of the last few days of sunshine to dry out rough-hewn lumber and stack it into a small mountain behind his store. Late every afternoon, the Swedes passed logs one at a time along a human chain, as they would buckets of water for fighting a fire, with the last two men wielding the hammers. The schoolhouse took shape before my eyes, reminding me of the speed with which gallows can be erected. Miraculously, from the chaos of boards emerged a defined floor. Lo and behold, there was enough space for several large tables.

Lars said the school would be easy enough to expand as more students arrived. With the floor done, the men fashioned leftover lumber into benches and stools. Large window openings with barn-door-style shutters would suffice for the summer. Already everyone referred to the school so naturally you would have thought it grew out of the ground like the never-ending supply of evergreens surrounding us. To both Lars and Father, this looming frame was welcome evidence of civilization rising in the wilderness. They still discussed each detail of their enterprise as though it advanced as planned, even as Father had to stop the conversation to gasp for air.

Young people can be idiots. I was one, and perhaps if Father had made the decision to follow the waves when he first thought of coming here, he would have eventually ascertained that he was one. The day we sailed, I stood resolute at the helm with eyes intent on the western horizon, willing myself to discern land still thousands of miles away. No one could picture how interminably the voyage stretched across the Atlantic, how deadening the drone of a freshwater steamer sounded hour after hour, how the trip by rail to northwestern Ontario—a place so many times bigger than all of Britain—rattled a body to the marrow. Grief is not always caused by a random outside force visited upon the innocent; it can be actively solicited by manifestly stupid decisions. I should have twigged there was something wrong with a place where land was being given away. England's problems were dwarfed by the magnitude of this monstrous country. After two years here in Wabigoon, Father, whether he granted it or not, had evidently come to the conclusion that he did, after all, make a mistake, and wanted to follow Mother into the grave. I did not blame him.

Lars Larsen was neither disappointed with his new country nor prone to complaints of any sort. He was a stalwart man, blond, with something of the Nordic bearing in his broad shoulders and ruddy, angular face. Even without knowing him I would easily remark his solid stock. Just as the sun rose every morning, so would Lars pull on his roughly knit sweater and overalls to open his store. I could hear his friends and relatives back home talking about him as their reliable Swede in Canada. If your wagon wheel broke or your boat sank or your pump jammed, he was the one to call for help. To him, the future was bright, no matter what kind of atrocious punishment rained down on him in his all-weather rubber boots. Energetic and helpful, interested in whatever topic I raised, he presented a picture I felt guilty criticizing. I certainly understood the need to be neighbourly out here in the bush, and hoped they did not find me superior.

He installed us in what I would have called a rough tool shed back in England. There was nothing personal in it, though, since all the other shacks were exactly the same. Class distinction fell on desolate soil in this country because survival in uniformly rough circumstances depended on other standards. Money made paltry difference in a place where there was little to buy. Hardship was instead displaced by the ability to hunt, fish, or chop wood.

And yet, despite the fact that Father and I lived hundreds of miles away from any real civilization, we were updated regularly on the news of the nation. Knowing the train would drop off newspapers for Lars at his store each day, I found myself listening for its plaintive whistle. I pretended it was the lament of a lost, homesick loon trying to find its way back home. Some days I was tempted to answer out loud but so far had succeeded in checking myself. I did not want to loosen into a madwoman's wail and unnerve my fellow villagers. Instead, I answered the call with my feet, silently rushing across the several hundred yards of mud to Lars's store, where I scooped up my *Manitoba Daily Free Press* and hugged it tight to my chest as I hastened back to our shack and pored over the day's treasures. On my wobbly stool, pulled up to the plank table Father hammered together when he was fit and robust, I indulged my imagination in tales of the civilization I had lost in coming to this sorry place.

Articles ranged from the frivolous to the sublime, all jumbled up sumptuously in my pot of reading material. I gorged on luscious details of fêtes, hoop skirts, polished floors, and rich chamber music. I devoured reviews of plays I would never see, lectures on science, philosophy, and literature I would never hear. Thinking of these far-off places, I boarded a train, and with no effort at all could feel its determined thrust under my feet. We barrelled through wilderness for hours, even days, before the flow of undifferentiated green outside the window finally broke into roads and homes and shops, and I was ushered into the embrace of bustling crowds, oh yes, where I hailed a horse and buggy and was hurried off to my exciting evening engagement—until I was stopped short by a sigh I perceived as my own. Desperate not to awaken Father, I quietly gulped in news from around the world with a longing for something other than where I was, even who I was. Father would not have recognized me on this side of British reserve.

One day there was a history piece on the invention of the telegraph in America that overnight in '61 rendered the Pony Express obsolete.

I imagined the Pony Express rider on the day he went into the stable for his horse, expecting to put in his usual honest day's work to feed his family. I saw him saddling up to deliver the mail when his boss came to tell him to collect his gear and go home. What did he do? He had to adapt. The way we all must.

Father and I distracted ourselves daily by reading and talking about Louis Riel. From the information I could cobble together, Riel was a different kind of rebel from his American counterpart of a hundred years before. The American rebel was the quintessential hothead son, especially sensitive to unjust treatment and prone to racing off with a swarm of fellow citizens to make some sort of public ejaculation. Apparently constitutionally unsuited to compromise, the American version was more prone to railing on about the principle of the thing before dumping perfectly good cargo into the sea and burning gruesome effigies. Lest one think him worn out, he would rise up the next day, prepared to do it all over again. In the long tradition of Britons bludgeoning each other, he contributed the innovation of guerrilla warfare by taking to the forest and popping out when his father's redcoats went by. And so the American sons chased the patriarch's henchmen all the way back to England.

Loyalist siblings faced with the same unreasonable father chose instead to bite their tongues and remove themselves north. While life up here might have been a bit more rustic, it offered plenty of room to enjoy the full warmth of their royal father's approbation. Now, more than a century later, Louis Riel rose as a new kind of son disgruntled with the empire. In his Métis incarnation, he was an adoptive cross between the Natives who were here first and the French who were conquered by Wolfe. In America, the royal father had to change his taxing ways or lose his son; in Canada, Riel issued ultimatums to his oppressive mother, the queen: either leave him alone or make him a partner in the family business.

Reading about Riel every day, I found myself thinking about these rebels. What did they do all day as I chopped vegetables for stew or swept the floor under Father's bed? Did they debate the future and make their battle plans, or were they absorbed by the more mundane business of cleaning their guns and hunting for food?

—When you get better, Father, I said as I filled the teapot, you might want to create a history lesson from all these articles.

I turned to Father with a smile, pointing to the pile of papers that lay unread on his lap. He was propped up on the pillows and folded blankets I had arranged under him. Knowing I expected a response, he picked up a newspaper and read out a headline.

—"Riel Openly Defies the Queen's Authority."

He looked at me as though the very meaning of the headline was incomprehensible to him, and then shivered. As I picked up a shawl to drape over his shoulders, he waved me off and worked himself into a coughing fit. Valiantly, when he finished coughing, he offered,

—Mr. Riel evidently does not realise the lengths to which the British will go to defend their monarch.

I dampened a cloth and dabbed it across his forehead to relieve the sweat that had popped up from his efforts. I thought I could discern a faint gurgle at the end of his expired breaths.

—He must realise it, Father, I said gently. He was educated in Montreal by Jesuits, whom I can only assume would have come across the British. He must have some sort of plan.

He laid his head back on the pillow and closed his eyes.

—This railway is a feat of engineering genius that will not be stopped by a few hundred malcontents.

Father wanted to stay connected to the world. I thought that a good sign. As long as he kept fighting, he could come through this. It was a nasty illness, but he was a strong, vital man. So long as he still cared to read our articles and talk about the world, he remained determined. This was the adventure he had dreamed about. Soon he would be back to his old self.

As Father lapsed into sleep once more, I tried to anticipate why anyone, rebel or soldier, would want to fight for this abhorrent place. The Métis must have known they were vastly outnumbered. If there was to be a showdown between a new nation bent on extending itself from sea to sea and those who would try to stop it, one would think there was a dramatic plan afoot. Perhaps Mr. Riel knew full well what he was doing and had some secret stratagem, or a store of weapons that would alarm Mr. Macdonald in Ottawa to the point of dissuading him from an open fight. If Mr. Riel did not have some brilliant plan, he shared with us the unfortunate position of being too far in to back out of a terrible mistake.

Why did sick people experience their worst moments shortly after midnight? A door seemed to open at the stroke of the clock, unleashing gothic forces determined to hound the worrisome into the terrifying. Father began a series of coughing fits that did not subside until dawn, when reinforcements of light crept in to settle him down. Exhausted, we lapsed into the kind of sleep that mimics falling backwards off a cliff. The sun was as high as it ever got in this northern clime when I eventually shook myself awake to make tea before Father stirred.

Father must have repeated my name several times before I heard his hoarse voice at my back. I turned around to face purposeful if watery blue eyes.

—What is it, Father?

—It is entirely possible that I may never recover from this.

—Do not talk like that! Of course you will recover.

—You need to run the school if I cannot.

—I will not permit you to think such morbid thoughts! Our agreement was that you would be the teacher, so do your part and get better.

He tapped his shaking finger gingerly on the table.

—I have come to understand what a good influence your mother was to hold me back from the rash decisions I am inclined by nature to make. We should accept our mistake, Abigail, and try to make the best of it. Your taking up my position here is the best you are going to do without me.

—This is not the time to make more decisions, Father. You have things out of perspective because you are sick. When you are on the mend and feel your energy back, all will look different. Spring is here. You are sure to improve.

I insisted on straightening up his bed as he looked on, gamely pretending to eat his oatmeal. Afterward, he let me fuss as I shaved him and washed his hair. Reclaiming order calmed us both. Once finished, I tucked him in, and fell into bed myself. Even as his shallow breaths organized themselves into regular breathing, I could not stave off rising panic. What if he never regained enough strength to work again? I could be teaching all day and nursing all night.

There would be no point in us being here. I needed to take him back to England, where he could at least be comfortable. Lars brought us here for his school. If Father could not fulfil his obligations in running it, would Lars's generosity extend to paying for us to go home? We had no other way of surviving out here. If he refused, perhaps I could appeal to relatives back home for passage money. How realistic was that? He would never survive the trip. I was trapped here no matter which solution I approached.

Lars dropped over more often now that Father was ill. He offered to reinforce the roof after the punishing winter, and to fill holes that opened up drafts between loosened wall boards, all measures Father and I would not have known to take. I could see the consternation on his face as he witnessed just how weak Father had become, which bothered me for all kinds of reasons. Be that as it may, I was still somewhat consoled by Father's invigorated interest when Lars announced his willingness to jump on the train at a moment's notice to go and fight for Macdonald.

—Lars, how can you be serious? I cried, looking to Father's strained face for support.

Lars looked disapprovingly at nails he was about to hammer, until he pounded them into compliance. Then, searching for his next board, he smiled pleasantly and held forth.

—This country hasn't forgiven what Riel did the last time. Tom Scott was one of the forty-eight hostages captured in the storming of Fort Garry in '69. Scott had more energy than all the other hostages put together to curse his captors day and night. He could think up insults that no one had ever contemplated before.

—He was Protestant, was he not, if he came from Ontario?

—And Riel was Catholic, Indian, and French. With that much raw material, and locked in a cell all day and night, Scott had plenty of time for creativity. From all reports, his cussing was as relentless as his determination to escape, which he managed to do several times.

For the first time in weeks, I smiled.

—He must have been quite a handful.

—The Métis take loss of face seriously, and the more irked the guards became the more vulgar Scott's improvisations grew. Maybe that was his own personal war strategy, or maybe it was his way of coping with what might lay in store for all of them, or maybe he was naturally an obnoxious personality. Whatever it was, Riel's men would tolerate no more from him. They held a court martial in the fashion of a buffalo hunt, and Riel presided over the vote to execute. The next day, they stood Scott in front of a firing squad and were done with him.

—He was executed for swearing?

—Ask any of the men who come into my store every day, and they will tell you it was cold-blooded murder—and Riel was the one in charge.

I looked over at Father for a reaction, but his head had wedged between the wall and his pillow as he had drifted back into the only retreat from misery open to him. Once Lars finished up his last board, he nodded gentlemanly to my offering of tea. Neither of us interfered with my clattering of the kettle and teapot, or the clinking of the spoon in his cup. Ordinarily I would have found his silence uncomfortable, except that I could tell he was working up to something.

—Your father is having a hard time of it.

—He is a fighter. He will come out of this.

He nodded slowly, leaning forward, elbows on his knees. He opened his hands as though in supplication to a higher force before clasping them back together. I wanted him to talk about Riel again, but he only sat up and rearranged the salt and pepper mills on our rough kitchen table.

—We have a prospector who hit a small stake over at Gold Rock last month. This is just the beginning of discoveries that will bring more people. Maybe not a full-blown rush, but enough to make us a thriving town.

He said "just" as "youst." In the face of his earnestness, I tried to drum up sincere interest in this desolate outpost. For all the help he had been to Father and me, and all he was yet willing to do, he deserved my appreciation. He seemed encouraged by my undivided attention.

—As your father knows, the men want to learn English. Others in town who already speak English want to learn how to read and write for the first time. Children will come later, but we need to open the school now so that everyone who comes to our town knows we have a place for their children.

Undoubtedly Lars went to sleep at night with his own freezing fantasies of one day exerting himself as mayor of a bustling and thriving Wabigoon.

—Father will be well again shortly.

—Maybe so, and we will hope for that. For now, the school is ready for students. All that is holding us up is not having a teacher. I took on the responsibility of getting one here in time, and the men were willing to provide their labour. They have fulfilled their side of the bargain.

What possible excuse would justify a refusal to step into Father's boots in the short-term? It behooved me to volunteer rather than force my own conscription. I could not expect Lars to understand a frivolous rejection of teaching just because I maintained illusions of a more adventurous life.

—I will step into the breach when you need me, Lars.

He nodded his thanks, relief flushing his lined face. When he got up to go, he shook my hand and looked directly into my eyes.

—I will tell the men we can open the school next week. When you need me, Abigail, I will return the favour.

Over the next few days, as I watched Lars come out of his store and plod across the mud toward our shack, I noticed he was more relaxed in tipping his hat toward me, as though already sure of me as an intimate. I worried he might harbour hopes of making a life with me here in this awful place, that he presumed some sort of tacit approval so long as he waited patiently. Was that why he dedicated himself to making things easier for us, why he brought provisions and firewood so reliably?

The Swedes applauded the day I stepped through the rough schoolhouse door to start their first class. I looked over faces shining with the belief that learning English would connect them to the future of their new country. Surmising I was more knowledgeable than I was, they asked me questions regarding land grants and other legal issues about which I had no special understanding.

Lars began to leave thoughtful gifts on what I absurdly called our porch. When I opened the door to find bits of candy and ribbon, my stomach sank. It irritated me, actually. Why could I not just open my door without having to acknowledge someone else's misplaced appreciation? He would likely have been shocked by my reaction to what I believed was a gesture of comity because of Father's illness and my apparently discernible loneliness and helplessness. Would he do that for someone merely because she taught in his school?

Lars furnished me with paper and inkpots he must have ordered weeks before for Father, all at his own expense. He stopped by to ask if I would like to give him a list of books to order through his store. I could order from any bookshop I wished—Toronto, New York, Chicago, anywhere. I told him I would consult with Father.

Teacher, nurse, wife, trapped in this backwoods. I was cornered everywhere I turned. Back home we had a small library, a market with all sorts of fresh foodstuffs, soft fabrics, music, theatre. There was nothing here but the wilderness and a handful of Swedes who could not speak English. Father was so right. We made a horrendous, disastrous mistake.

I went down to Lars's store for flour, moose meat, turnips, carrots, and potatoes, since the garden I managed to eke out behind our shack the year before yielded potatoes that lasted us no longer than January. Lucky for us there were others around here who knew enough to plant a bumper crop and sell the surplus to Lars.

As he packed my meagre provisions in the store, I diverted my attention to his wall display of rifles.

—You should get yourself one of those, he said.

—I cannot imagine why.

—You wouldn't have to buy this moose meat from me if you hunted your own.

—Oh my goodness, Lars. If I ever saw one of those creatures I would do just about anything else in the world but wait around to shoot it.

In fact, this past winter I encountered a moose right outside our shanty. The hulking beast stood motionless, haughty black eyes, steam puffing out its gigantic nostrils, its neck the girth of a man's torso holding up a torture rack of antlers. Even if I were to shoot it—and actually hit it—what would I do then?

He smiled as he wrapped.

—There are people here who would butcher for a percentage of the meat. It's not so hard as you think. Just go down the railway track and you'll soon find one. They stand waiting for the train because they think it has come for a fight. Conductors have to watch for them because they won't back down.

My laughter at the audacity of a moose fighting a train encouraged more stories about black bears coming out of hibernation angry and hungry enough to root through everything in their path—tools, wagon seats, bales of hay—eating all that is edible and inedible, later to heave up the indigestible bits.

—Bears have a much better sense of smell than we do, he said pleasantly. We might as well live in houses made of toothpicks.

—Then what stops them from breaking in?

Lars shrugged dramatically. He clearly enjoyed teasing me.

I lasted no more than two days before again venturing down to his store.

—Lars, I need a pair of solid men's boots. I refuse to hop like a bird through the muck now that spring is here.

I did not expect him to have a pair of my size already in stock, but my size was in proportion to a strapping young boy Lars would expect to be helping his father with the ubiquitous building projects in process. Lars laughed when I complained about men having the freedom to clomp through anything without worrying about mud on a hemline.

Ever the salesman, he suggested I order a pair of men's pants to go with the boots, and then throw in the gun. I knew he would talk about the gun. He was not one to bring up a topic and then forget about it. In fact, I had counted on him talking me into it. He told me a consolidated order now would be cheaper than one order now and a second one later. I hesitated, unsure of depleting the small pot of money that Father and I had left.

He reached up to the rack and pulled down one of the rifles.

—This is a Winchester. I hope one day they make it a bit lighter, but even as it is you can handle it easily enough.

He set it in my hands.

—But I have no intention of shooting anything.

—A gun is like a shovel to make a garden or a hammer to make a shelter. You grow into it.

Its weight and solidity in my hands felt serious. Thinking abstractly of the ability to take care of myself was quite different from having the concrete instrument in my hands. Quite suddenly, and with no lockstep line of logic, I was inflamed with desire for this gun. Lars said the Winchester had a lever action that required one to pull down the apparatus around the trigger in order to load a bullet from the magazine into the shooting chamber. The shell casings could be reused if I refilled them with a bullet and gunpowder. That would make the enterprise sufficiently cheap that even I could afford it. Or at least that was one of my mounting rationalizations.

Back in England, my interest in a gun would have prompted barely perceptible gasps. As I thought of myself here in the backwater of a continent with thousands of empty miles around me, I considered how England and Europe would look if the peasants had routinely owned guns. Despots would have faced more than just their aristocratic armies turning against them. We would soon find out, now that Switzerland had armed its population as a reserve army.

Alone in this New World, I had lived in perpetual panic until now. There was something in the autonomy of a gun that focused me. If man or country could not defend me, I might still defend myself.

—I will take it, I said to Lars, with a voice sounding, to my ears, as though it emanated from outside his door.

Two weeks later, I heard the train whistle blow its haunting lament, and ran down to Lars's store where he presented me with my brand new Winchester. I feigned only casual interest as I watched him deftly push the cartridge into the loading gate, load the chamber by swinging the lever down and up, pretend to fire, and then reload the chamber. He studied me out of the corner of his eye as I repeated his demonstrations. I tried to ignore his devotion to helping me.

My Winchester, it turned out, presented a personality of its own, sitting there behind the door as though waiting patiently for me to properly introduce it to a round of target practise. I had an inkling of why men gave names to their boats and ships. My gun was not shy, exactly, but reserved—aware of its own power and, as a result, with no need to show off. It was better described as mutedly insistent, since I could not go past the door without having my attention drawn to it. Maybe we named things that gave us power. I did not mind that. Power should have a name.

I had not shot it yet and was half afraid to try, even as I reviewed the steps Lars had taught me. Before I could use the cartridges, I had to be sure how to load them without the thing going off. Why should a gun, such a vile mechanism in so many hands, have rekindled my will to go on? All I could posit was that it convinced me that I could take some sort of action, a daft idea since I was not planning to do anything I could not have done before. But here was the thing: I never thought about venturing up into our rocky land behind the village, and now I found myself thinking about it all the time.

After Lars left and Father went back to sleep for the night, I searched my own soul for the reason I had a gun and what I planned to do with it. Nothing practical, and yet it invigorated me to think about shooting it. If I had been alive when the United States decided to separate from Britain, I deliberated about what I would have done. Even now, if I had been born Métis in Saskatchewan, would that be reason enough to sign up with Riel? I had never considered before what would impel me to fight. Would anything matter to me that much?

For the first time, I trampled a path through the bush out to our rocky back quarter. The Swedes were gone to the mine and would not need me until the afternoon. Snow still clung to the ground under bushes and evergreens, unwilling to pack up and leave despite having thoroughly worn out its welcome. The gun was lighter and smaller than I expected, even though I was sure the weight would soon feel exacting if I had to hold it up to my shoulder for any length of time. I strode in my new boots, extending my legs as long and far as they could go while a tingling sensation flowed down my arm and out into the gun. I did not know how I would ever again suffer the mincing steps necessary for a skirt to be a pleasing female garment. My boots stomped over the unforgiving rock as I kicked my skirt out in front of me, jolting it to keep ahead of my feet. Next time, I would wear the work trousers.

Incredibly, I relished the honest hardness of the terrain. In contrast to the treacherous furrows in town, nature was intact out here, in patches at least. If I stayed to the rocky perimeter of our plot, I could avoid the deeper snow clear back to the clutter of rock left by ancient glaciers. What a colossal thing a glacier must have been to suck up boulders the size of churches and dump them down willy-nilly in a rush of melting ice. The configuration of granite formed a rough cliff several stories high that would have made a magnificent waterfall had the glacier connected it to a body of water. As it was, scaling the dry waterfall took me up over the Laurentian Shield onto a corridor of rock with a small wall at the back, perfect for a target range. All was ringed by scrawny evergreen trees and bushes. I planned to squirrel away some empty cans to take up there for practise.

I did not fire anything, just sat and studied this contraption of wood and metal for a long time. I was building my courage to load it.

Father slept for the next two days straight. I read the newspaper enough times to almost recite every column. I was about to take out my gun when he called my name. Catapulted into tears as I ran to him, I had to repeat over and over that I was fine. Of course he repudiated my assurances: if everything was fine, why was I crying? He struggled to sit up in bed and let me feed him the moose stew I had thinned to a soup. I could only hope a bit of nutrition would help him gain strength.

I once read that that hair continues to grow even after death. It was not true, of course, more the stuff of gothic novels, but I caught myself thinking about it as I observed the propensity of Father's hair to grow in rampant contradiction to his body's weakness. As I shaved him, he rambled on about how he wanted me to buy a cow to insure us against privation. The capacity to produce our own milk, butter, and cheese would keep us fattened and in possession of trade-worthy items. I humoured him, noting that we could have one shipped on the CPR line to make Macdonald's train useful for something other than soldiers. We remembered the cows outside the train window in the Lakehead when we first came here, an oddly domestic sight in the wilderness. I could not bear to tell him we may not be able to manage the price of a cow now that I had spent our money on a gun. I mused about whether I could learn to hunt.

I saw from the newspaper there was rioting in Ireland. Immigrants around here whose roots reached back to the Catholics of Ireland were the ones most likely to relish Riel's anti-England and anti-Orangemen sentiments. The Americans, too, were rather cheerful about turmoil here. I remembered in England hearing that American papers revelled in any troubles happening in Canada. They still had their noses out of joint that Britain managed to hold them back from their manifest destiny to spread over the entire continent. On this side of the ocean, we had all fallen into each other's histories.

I once read that people sometimes rally just before they expire, like a star waxing feverish in the process of burning out. I made the mistake of thinking this when Father rallied and ate a bit. His effort to rouse himself evidently pulled a plug that drained every last ounce of energy out of him. Soon he lay suspended between sleep and unconsciousness. He had such a kind face. As I watched him sleep, I remembered being too small to reach a shelf or learn a sum. He would carefully place his pipe on his book, place the book on his chair, and amble over to wherever I wanted him. If I needed help in a hurry, Mother was the one to call, but if I just needed to know help would be there eventually, no matter the obstacle, I would call him. He was much more patient than I would ever be.

I read aloud to Father about a new insurrection. In truth, I read to a hebetudinous figure deathly still in his bed. It had become my habit to hover my hand over his mouth to check that he was still breathing. At least coughing told me he was still with me.

In Battleford, a Cree Indian chief called Poundmaker was reputed to support Riel. He had gathered together five hundred warriors on the hills around that town, with more arriving from all over. Frightened women and children were huddled into a barracks only two hundred yards square. The cries of children must have rung out in the cold, empty wilderness. A mere handful of soldiers braced to fend off hostile forces that amassed around them, with an attack said to be imminent. Poundmaker would soon need to come into Battleford for supplies.

As I was reading aloud to myself, Lars's familiar tap sounded at the door.

—I see you have your father on the edge of his seat, he said as he took his place at the kitchen table. He knew all about Battleford.

—They say a great war is brewing, he said, one that will unite the Indians and half-breeds.

—Macdonald is sending General Middleton out with thousands of troops. Do you think it will truly take only a few days to make the railway ready? It says here that the railway tracks are not yet all connected.

Lars nodded leisurely several times. Either he was taking time to think through his answer, or just enjoying the fact that he had been asked a question in the first place.

—Van Horne knows what he's doing. He moved troops all over the states during the Civil War. The north shore of Lake Superior will be his biggest challenge, but he's lucky there is still enough ice to lay temporary track. Even with Chinese workers and sleighs, the recruits might have to do some walking.

In my mind's eye, I reeled at the spectacle of this gigantic movement of men and animals west. The job of feeding the men alone required 75,000 pounds of food to be moved, not to mention the 775,000 pounds of forage for the livestock that pulled the wagons to bring the food. Some said this grand show of force was simply to frighten all the Indians across the country by giving them a sample of what they were up against if they chose to collude.

And so, just as Poundmaker trapped the women and children of Battleford, Middleton would soon trap Poundmaker. If Riel did not have a war strategy that included widespread coalition, he too would soon enough be surrounded.

I gave a name to my place on the other side of the dry waterfall, the one place I did not feel trapped: the Range. In this new country, everything was given new names, whether Indian words with their murmuring vowel sounds or names imported from Britain meant to animate the landscape into some concordance with what existed an ocean away. I liked the name "Range" because it was stripped down to its function, or what I hoped would be its function once I took the plunge by loading and firing.

I took an axe and twine to fashion myself a rough ledge where I could place my target cans. There was a pile of fallen tree trunks near a clutch of evergreens that would provide all the lumber I needed. Back in England, I would have sought a bench or stump on which to sit and ponder existence. Here, I marched around the perimeter to stake out ground sufficiently level to support construction. Safety was unlikely to present itself as an issue, since I would not meet up with anyone back here, although you never knew where or when you might bump into small groups of Indians travelling about. As the village filled up with more immigrants, the bustle drew Indians to it like a magnet, whether for trade or out of mere curiosity.

Everyone knew the local Indians who frequented Lars's store. There were barely a hundred who lived close by, with names like Little Gull, Six Fingers, Indian Jack, Big Squaw, Mrs. Parenteau, and Anneway Keesick. For the first time, I reflected on how they got their names, whether they chose them on their own or if the immigrants merely pronounced what they could. As I understood it, we were situated at the junction of two large tribes that were variations of the same nation. The Americans used the term *Chippewa* for the group living to the south and spread over Wisconsin and Minnesota. Then, to the north into Canada, the name changed to *Ojibwa*, indicating people who were shorter in stature, as though living evidence of a harsher climate that stunted growth. What did they say about us? What did they say about Riel?

Lars updated me that the situation at Battleford had brightened—good news since one third of the Indian population of the entire North was now concentrated there. No attack had happened yet. The Blackfoot tribe's decision to remain loyal to Canada was being rewarded by Ottawa with a promise of settling disputed land claims soon. There were so many dispatches coming in, it was difficult to tell which were accurate and which arose from jittery speculation.

Sometimes at night I held my breath when I heard ghastly silence from Father's bed. For murderous moments, I starved myself of oxygen in the hopes that my gasping for breath would impel him over whatever obstacle prevented him from getting there on his own. I was frantic to find him a doctor. Lars promised to bring the one scheduled to pass through town within the next week or two.

One morning, Father did not backslide into sleep right away, but called me to his bedside and took my hand.

—Abigail, we must talk about your future.

—There is lots of time for my future.

—We must look at our situation squarely. I am not going to last much longer.

—You are exhausted and demoralized. The doctor will be here any day to tell you this was an especially bad case of pneumonia.

—I have been thinking you should marry Lars.

—What?!

—He has clearly taken a shine to you. You need someone to take care of you when I am gone.

—Do not talk such rubbish, Father. I am perfectly capable of taking care of myself.

—He will work that store up, perhaps build an inn in time. He is an enterprising man, that Lars. You could do worse.

—I do not want to get married any more than I want to teach, Father.

Confusion eclipsed his face. He cocked his head as though trying to decipher a foreign language.

—Why? What else would you do out here alone?

As he slumped back on his pillow, I conceded and sat down beside him on the bed. Taking up his hand to warm in mine, I was surprised how papery and old his skin had become.

—Not let you give up, that is what I am going to do.

—I should never have pressed you to come here.

—It was as much my decision.

—But you—

—Enough about me. We are both going to be fine. It is time for you to get some sleep.

Unable to resist the onslaught of fatigue, he was soon insensible to his worries once more. In the half-light of his illness day after day, he must have spent hours wracking his brain for solutions to our predicament, knowing there was not enough money to build what we needed and not enough health to do anything about it.

The next day, I walked across the Range to line myself up with the shelf where I set up my cans. It was the height of presumptuousness for me to think I might hit a can on purpose. All the same, I fit the cartridge into the chamber, hiked the butt end of the rifle up into my shoulder, aimed in the general direction of the target area, and pulled the trigger. I had braced myself for an aggressive kick in response to the firing, but my expectation was overblown. What I did not foresee, and therefore what startled me into my scream and subsequent fall, was the sound of the explosion.

The crack of the rifle was one I would have expected from a metal mountain dropping onto a giant rock. To anyone watching, my tumble would have resembled that of a circus clown. Still, I would wear with deep satisfaction the bruising from my elbow to my shoulder that I could feel becoming pulpy. That sound of the gun, the sudden and insistent bark of an inhuman beast, became even more powerful as I remembered it. I reinvented myself as more courageous with every recollection of it.

ELECTRIFIED

Day after day, I hopped out of bed already thinking of the Range. I weighed the likelihood of Father having sensed something different about me. One morning I grabbed my cloak and covered my Winchester with it in case Lars was out and about. Although his pointers were inevitably helpful, I wanted to make my mistakes and feel like mistress of my own gun. These days I could get up to the Range in thirty minutes if I walked quickly. By the time I hauled myself up the boulders, I was usually puffing. No matter. The exertion was a distraction at the least, and arguably made me strong.

I picked up the cans knocked off the shelf where I set my targets the day before. The mess struck me as slightly odd, considering that the weather had been unusually clear and still overnight. Perhaps a bear lumbered through, or a moose, despite my careful washing of the cans to leave no smell of food. I stood cogitating for several seconds when, not ten feet from me in the trees, a horse whinnied softly. I was too startled to think, no less move.

The horse swung its head around to look directly into my face, deep chestnut eyes with a white star on the ebony hide between its eyes. Apparently impatient, it bobbed its head up and down, snorting. I followed the movement until my gaze swept down low enough to see what it was trying to show me.

The horse stood over the crumpled heap of a man on the ground. A large-brimmed hat close by had what looked like dried blood encrusted on the inside band, prompting me to crouch down and inspect more closely to find that the man's head was injured. The horse whinnied once more before flicking its nose upward as though enjoining me to get busy and do something. In unthinking acquiescence, I stepped closer to the stranger until I noticed pistols in the holsters strapped around his waist.

My mind logjammed with the impossibility of this lump of flesh and dirty clothing actually lying at my feet. How ugly he was. One could not gouge wrinkles this deeply in a short span of time. This was the kind of face set so long in its crabbed expression that the sun had baked it into permanence. His face must have been a furrowed trail of cussed thoughts that accrued over a lifetime, the work of a miserable soul from the beginning to what now looked like the end of his days. A scar dragged his lips into a sneer. Pinkish foam gathered at one corner of his mouth. Something must have been bleeding inside. The horse whinnied, threw up its head, and began pawing the ground. The rifle in the saddle pack stood out as impressively bigger and heavier than mine.

—Settle down, now, I told it, holding up one hand.

It was stupid to think the beast understood me, but something in my tone or action must have conveyed good will because he calmed himself. My mind sped to an article I once read on Louis Pasteur and his germ theory, reminding me to take extra care not to touch anything with my bare fingers. I dabbed away the foam with my handkerchief before opening the cowboy's beaten-up leather jacket to a denim shirt so faded and worn it had frayed through in places. Around his side was a splotch of black dried blood broken by a trickle of bright red at the bottom of the shirt. His belt buckle and boots looked marginally newer than his jacket.

His thinning hair and wiry grey beard rendered him indistinguishable from most of the riffraff in Wabigoon, although, so far as I knew, most were not strapped with pistols. Calling on the deepest spring of my own humanity, poised to bolt, I defied Pasteur's germs to stretch out my hand and feel the man's forehead.

—We have a fever here, I told the horse in the tone of a doctor addressing a family member. He is dry but with the temperature of a fully stoked oven.

The horse dropped its face close to mine. The deduction took a moment to knock on my mind's still partially closed door.

—A fever means he is not dead.

The horse closely tracked my movements as I poured water out of the canteen and into my cupped hand to wet the man's lips. I soaked my handkerchief more thoroughly and formed it over his forehead.

—I will try to get his temperature down, I said. Then I will fill one of those wider cans over there with water for you.

I had become used to speaking aloud to mute bodies, and the sound of my own voice encouraged me. The horse was apparently unwilling to walk away from the fallen rider to forage. Once I soaked the blood-caked shirt and carefully pulled the sticky fibres loose, I could see the torn and ragged wound, a hole unable to close properly because it had not been stitched, yet the blood was clotting well enough. All I could tell was that the blood, seeping as it did with the slightest application of pressure, showed no sign of infection. I made a mental note to bring disinfectant from the shack. Its application would sting unbearably, incentive for him to surface to consciousness if he were anywhere close.

Without knowing the bullet's entry point, I had no way to assess how likely he was to survive. As I glanced up at the horse, I spied a coiled rope strapped to the saddle.

—You are going to help me turn him over.

Slowly, I unstrapped the rope to tie one end to the side of the saddle and the other end to the cowboy's belt. The horse indulged me a couple of steps to shift the man's weight and expose his side and part of his back. Once I loosened his shirt at the back to get a good look, I saw that something had obviously entered from the back where his shirt was ripped and bloody.

—It appears he has an exit wound, I said.

The horse stared at me.

—He might escape an infection if there is no lead in him.

The horse's eyes were large, expectant pools of black. I washed the wound as best I could, and brought the last of my water to the animal.

—You look uncomfortable, I told him. I'm just going to unbuckle your saddle. You are all squashed together in a girdle with that strapped around your middle.

The horse cooperated by standing still, so long as my movements remained fluid, slow, and manifestly well intentioned. I slid the heavy load down onto the ground without touching the rifle.

—There is nothing more I can do, I said to the horse.

No pawing of the ground, no throwing back his head and whinnying—it just stared with those huge, liquid eyes. I stooped to pick up my rifle and marched over to the Range.

—This morning I came here to set up my three cans, and nothing is going to stop me from doing just that. A body can cope with only so much.

I lined up my barrel with the middle can, careful to analyze how much I needed to compensate for the position of my sightline compared to the barrel of the gun, shifting around several times to get things just right. When I pulled the trigger, you would never have known there was a bullet in the gun. I had no idea where the shot had gone. There had not even been the sound of a ricochet, so it must have just sailed up and over the rock shelf.

—You see? I shouted, pounding back to the horse. Obviously I need to practise, and you are distracting me. He is just lying there, and there is nothing more I can do.

Well, that was a lie. I could have run and found Lars. He would have recruited the Swedes, and all would soon be tromping through my business right up to my Range, the one place in the world where I should have been able to be alone.

—All right, I said, throwing my hands up over my head as though caught out for something.

I put down my rifle and dragged the saddlebag over. As I did so, the horse made those guttural sounds that reminded me of eating something comforting, like pancakes with butter and warm, golden syrup.

—Well, glad you are happy. Maybe you can explain to me why I am suddenly obligated to save this sorry excuse for a man? He gets himself into trouble with his guns, gets himself shot, collapses on my Range, and I am supposed to pick up the pieces to make him better?

I lodged the saddlebag under the man's head as a pillow. Angry, I grabbed my gun, clomped back to my shooting position, pulled back the butt end of the rifle to my shoulder, and shot without thinking. The middle can flew off its perch.

I could hear my own gasp.

—Did you see that!? I demanded.

Talking to that horse was like talking to a wall.

—You do not seem to understand. I have never done that before. The horse stared placidly as though he had seen this many times which, now that I thought about it, he most likely had. I felt conciliatory.

—I will cover him up, I said magnanimously.

The bedroll must have kept the man warm so far. He was travelling in temperatures still frigid most of the time despite the fluctuations heralding spring. For insurance, I spread my cloak down over top of his bedroll.

I ran back to pick up the gun in a spirit of celebration, swung it up to my shoulder, and shot again. Miraculously, I hit the second can, and then the third. Breathless with excitement, I turned to the horse.

—Something has happened to me!

Insensible to anything beyond the sound of the horse's breathing and mine, I listened to the world that had for miles and miles around silenced itself for a moment. The sun tracked across the sky, and I breathed these particular breaths that I would never breathe again. While this inert figure lay on the ground, a life hanging in the balance, I could barely contain my elation. Perhaps some bargaining for my conscience was in order.

—Look, tomorrow I will bring disinfectant and bandages, maybe even Lars. You must be getting hungry. You can forage around here for now and do the best you can. I will bring you food and water.

Later, sitting back home with Father's endless sleeping, I vowed to stop lamenting my poor fortune and turn my thoughts toward action. I settled upon enlisting Lars's help in the morning, and sleep came with my repeated recollection of metal hitting metal.

Next morning, when Father awoke, he announced he was ready to eat a horse. I jumped to heat his soup, flooded with gratitude—for what, exactly, I was not quite sure, except that busywork often substitutes for sleep as an effective distraction from one's problems. Next to Father, the cowboy was easier to ignore. I noticed that passing time had the effect of diminishing my resolve to recruit Lars.

Lars's reaction took shape in my mind. He would speak louder, the way he did when he talked about Riel, as he listed the steps to be taken in reporting the incident. He would need to make a trip to Kenora—*he* would make the trip because now this was *his* cowboy—to arrange for the North-West Police to accompany him back. If this stranger turned out to be a prospector, logger, or trader who had encountered some sort of accident, perhaps injuring himself and getting back on his horse, they could notify next of kin to come and pick him up. But if he turned out to be shot, like I was fairly certain he was, judging from the size and nature of his guns, the excitement would only involve more people.

There was no doctor in town to see Father, which meant there was no doctor to see anyone else. In addition to the fact that Lars had no more space in his shack, moving someone wounded, especially over such rough terrain, would probably make him worse. Even if the cowboy were placed under house arrest, Lars would call on me to do the nursing, since I was already doing it with Father. Lars would add that I was good at it. Now that I thought of it, Lars had already told everyone about my shooting. If the cowboy died without regaining the capacity to affirm what happened to him, and although it might be stretching the bounds of possibility, some might surmise I was the one to be taken off to the North-West Police for questioning. Father could not survive without me.

Lars assumed Father and I were predictable entities—Father the frail and doting patriarch and me the spinster teacher. If I were not careful, if I made myself appear odd or sneaky or unpredictable, Lars would become suspicious of us. Including him in this mystery would give him new keys to my prison, which could well wind up the brick and mortar variety. If I thought Lars capable of keeping quiet about a single event that occurred in this town, I might have trusted him with a problem or two. I felt incensed at Lars and territorial about this intruding, wounded cowboy.

An unconscious body could not be interrogated. The best plan had to be going up and seeing what kind of condition he was in now. Lars could always be a backup plan.

As I struggled for calm, I missed Mother so deeply I could hardly breathe. Our home was soft cottons and tea biscuits, chocolate and oranges at Christmas. There were piano recitals, unexpected visitors, and laughing voices at impromptu parties. Most, I remembered her grey eyes with the special power of enlarging everything she loved. There was nothing more exhilarating than running home from school with grandiose plans, whether they be chasing whales with Ishmael or stowing away on a merchant ship in search of Crusoe's island. Instead of dismissing my whims with a shake of her head or an admonition to get on with something sensible, she inevitably reassured by stoking the tale with her own kindling.

Our imaginations roared through the rolling of dough for biscuits and the basting of the roast already in the oven until Father came home and called us the Brontës for spinning mundane details into epic adventures. We were a troupe of actors, the three of us, inventing our own settings and costumes, characters and plots, heartbreak and inspiration. I was an only child in a home where all was malleable and possible.

I wanted to stay with these comforting images even as my mind dragged me back to the morning she awoke with a vague pain in her side, the sort of discomfort we all get at one time or another that disappears soon after we get up and move about. Reality seeped into our world through niggling and persistent details. The pain became more pointed, day after day, whether we encouraged her to move about in a garden of doleful mists or happy sunshine, whether we fed her tea spiked with spices or sugar, whether we warmed her with a down coverlet or cooled her with the bracing freshness of an opened window. As she slid into listlessness, her ashen face retreated from me as though sinking in water, silent, calm, unbearably remote. Like Snow White, she lay unconscious amid sheets bleached in the sunshine, her plait of hair draped neatly over the shoulder of her crisp white night dress. All the care in the world could not make her better.

One morning toward the end, I noticed tears streaming down her face.

—What is it, Mother? I whispered, bending close to her. Are you in pain?

—My regret overtakes me.

—Regret? What regret could you possibly have? You are everything to Father and me.

Her lovely face smiled weakly as I dabbed her tears with her handkerchief.

—I have lived within a very small compass.

—You have kept a happy home!

—I wonder what I might have done, where I might have gone, had I the fortitude to live out even a small part of my imagination. I have really never ventured beyond my front gate.

These were the last words she said to me before lapsing into unconsciousness. I refused to leave her room, lying on the bed stroking her hair and face, staring out her window, taking up her crocheting to finish the tablecloth she had been working on for months. I waited for her to wake up and explain what it was about the life she chose that was such a disappointment. How could she be someone other than who I knew her to be?

As I paced her room during the day, I began to take note of the books in her bookcase. She was always in the midst of reading, but the specific book of the moment never struck me as particularly important. I pulled down a title, *Roughing It in the Bush* by Susanna Moodie. Although I never remembered her mentioning it, the pages looked well worn. I lay beside her on the bed as she faded, imagining how she might have read these tales through the lens of what I now knew.

Mrs. Moodie was not exactly the kind of adventurer I would call a hero. For a pioneer, she whined a great deal. I could see how my mother would identify with her background. Educated, intellectual, with dreams arising from a literary imagination, Mrs. Moodie risked travelling with her family halfway around the world to a Canadian backwater. Out in the bush, she had all the hardships I now found familiar—the weather, the people, the relentless parade of hardships inherent in a rustic life. Mother could envy this way of living only because she had never done it. It would have been as awful for her as it was for me.

I wished I had never found that ill-advised book. I wished Mother had never confessed her regrets to me. She did so at a time when I was discombobulated, prone to acting on my thoughts. Simple impulsiveness can easily be mistaken for courage to pursue a path not taken, if one is inclined to regret. Inevitable disasters befell Mrs. Moodie in her bush through fire, weather, sickness, even deaths of those around her. A thousand miles further inland, my bush produced disasters through ludicrous weather, a sick father, an overly earnest neighbour, and a stupid cowboy. I had already trumped Mrs. Moodie on the whining front.

If we could have waved a magic wand, Mrs. Moodie and I would surely have chosen to pop back into our safe beds in England. Mother was better off for her cowardice. Within her cramped compass, her regrets were mercifully circumscribed. My regrets had achieved epic proportions, and I was apparently not yet done.

After we buried Mother, Father and I sank into our respective bogs of grief. We left Mother's tasks undone. Dishes remained stacked on the countertops, as though in expectation of a thorough cupboard cleaning. Bread and cheese crumbs endured on the cutting board from one mealtime to the next. We chipped off bits of food as eating sporadically occurred to us. When the cheese remonstrated with mould growth, we simply chucked it in the garbage and replaced it. The kettle was always warm, but sometimes the tea leaves in the pot did not change from morning until night. I read Mrs. Moodie's book over and over, paying little attention to what Father might be doing.

A month after the funeral, when we found ourselves together at the kitchen table, Father placed in my hand what I assumed was a pocket watch, with its silver case, lacy engravings, and a door that sprang open when I pressed the finial on top. Rather than time, I soon beheld, it marked direction, a compass that at that moment firmly pointed west. I turned it over to discover an inscription: *So that you can always find your way back to me*. I looked into Father's benevolent face for an explanation.

—Your mother gave it to me as a gift when we were your age.

—Were you going somewhere?

—I had signed onto a merchant ship bound for Canada.

—You were going to be a sailor?

—You would not have been surprised back then. As a young man I had a thirst for adventure, and your mother knew it.

—But you never went.

—I decided my heart was more important than adventure. She might have married someone else by the time I returned, if I ever did.

—And so you stayed and became a teacher.

—Your mother loved home. I would not subject her to what I knew would make her unhappy.

If Mother had not told him of her regret, I was certainly not going to do so. There was no point in robbing him of whatever comforting thoughts he had left. Still, it left me to ruminate about what the lesson was in doing right by a loved one. Had Father pressed her beyond her natural reticence, she might have avoided a deathbed regret, but who was to say she would not have racked up twenty more once she realised where she had wound up.

Bit by bit, we pulled furniture around for the sake of a handy footstool while reading or a better view of the window where the sun would eventually sink into night. With no expectation of company, there was no need to return anything to its proper placement. Two months later, Father called me to the kitchen table, where he had spread out pamphlets about Canada over top the crumbs.

—I have been in touch with a merchant in northwestern Ontario. He has made me an offer to set up a school there.

As Father summarized the details, he drew an invisible map with his fingers over the tabletop. Here was the store in a small village now booming with pioneers who had come to mine and log. Many of the immigrant labourers did not speak English but wanted to learn. More, they wanted a school, especially now because their families were beginning to join them. This fellow, Lars Larsen, seemed a responsible civic leader who wanted to prepare for the future. He offered passage and accommodation for both Father and me, and a small stipend for Father to plan, establish, and run the school. We would be eligible for a land grant if we took an interest in constructing small buildings or raising a few cows or sheep.

—What do you think? he asked.

The memory of a young man's dream brightened his eyes, but his sagging face evinced an older man suffering loss.

—It is a long way to go to do the same old thing.

The look of disappointment sweeping over his face was unbearable to me.

— . . . but that does not mean the venture is impossible.

—What would make you happy, Abigail, if you could do anything?

No matter how honest one was with oneself, there was no crystal ball for how a speculation might turn out.

—That is an impossible question for me to answer, Father. Something I have never done before?

—Good! I will have our expenses covered. You can do as you please.

I envisioned myself becoming someone like Mrs. Moodie, having my adventure in the bush and then writing about it. I might learn how to build something, or start up a store or other kind of business. Maybe I could become a newspaper woman. I came to the conclusion that everything on this side of the ocean reminded me of loss, and everything on the other side promised unexplored possibility. Mother must have told me what she did to help me avoid a life mistake. I was susceptible to the idea that I should be courageous.

Dusk oozed around us in that hazy time just before a candle needs lighting, when we think we see things clearly even as they become obscured by shadow. Father and I sat at the table weighing a future we could foretell down to its finest details against another we could only speculate about in large brush strokes. I extended my hand across the table. Slowly, Father took it up, and covered my hand with his own.

—Let us do it, I whispered in the pitch-dark.

I once thought myself similar to Mother because she was sensible. If that were the case, how did I explain, now that I was on the other side of the ocean, my yearning for a gun instead of a husband? Mother found happiness elusive because she avoided risk. I became the adventurer and still nothing made me happy. I exasperated myself. Maybe happiness was not what I assumed it was.

When Father went back to sleep after breakfast, I left the shack with my rifle and a shovel, in case I had to dig a grave. The pack strapped onto my back contained Father's leftover porridge, carrots for the horse, bandages, and disinfectant. I gloried in the wild image I cut. If I ever encountered myself in the bush, I was sure I would be terrified. I had made a decision. Lars was not going to get my Range or the cowboy.

Even before I climbed over the crest of the stone waterfall, I could hear the horse's rebuking neigh.

—Mind your own business, I called back to him stupidly. What else did I expect this horse to do?

The horse's obvious indignation had not been sufficient to move him off the protective vigil he maintained over the man still lying exactly where I left him. Approaching gingerly, I offered the horse a carrot, gratified by the munching that ensued. I picked up my cloak and folded it, then rolled up the cowboy's bedroll. I nudged his boot with my foot. Nothing. Kneeling beside him, I set my rifle down beside the shovel.

This time, when I knelt down to perform my triage, the horse stepped out of my way. I kept my attention on the cowboy, starting with an assessment of his breathing, which he was still doing, albeit shallowly. All the blood had now dried into a black crust, suggesting a healing process. Now that I thought of it, the bit of bloody foam I observed when I first saw him was gone. If the bullet had nicked part of his lung, it might be healing. As an afterthought, I reached my hand out to feel his forehead.

Before I could touch him, my arm was grabbed instantly in a vice grip. Steel blue eyes glared at me an inch from my face. His lightning stare flashed for a split second before he collapsed back down, passed out from the effort, his arm limp, his head turned to the side.

My heart pounded right up into my mouth, transfixing me for several minutes. The next time I reached out to feel his forehead, he stayed put. Still a fever. The horse pawed the ground beside me, maybe able to read something that I could not in the cowboy's harrowing clench, urging me to hurry and do something. This loathsome man had somehow managed to train an absurdly loyal horse.

I repeated my ministrations from the day before, except this time I doused his wounds with disinfectant. He must have lapsed into deep unconsciousness because he did not flinch. After cooling his forehead with my compress and encouraging drops of water into his mouth from my cloth, I fed the horse the leftover oatmeal the cowboy clearly was not ready to eat. Since there was nothing more I could do for him, I turned my attention to shooting. All the while I practised, time stood still. I lived in a moment of absolute concentration when my mind and body were in complete agreement. No other mental chatter penetrated the vault of my attention, a simple and compelling pleasure profound in its glorious peace.

If the cowboy lived long enough, I could bring the doctor back to the Range. But for good reason Lars would find it absurd to drag a poor doctor up a waterfall of rock. Even if I changed my mind and wanted to tell Lars about the cowboy, I had no way of carrying it off at this point. If I said I discovered an injured man just this morning, I would face questions like *What makes you think he's getting better? Why does the horse know you?* If I said that I discovered an injured man the other day but thought I would just leave him to see if he died or got up and rode away, I would appear to have taken leave of my senses. I knew from my schoolchildren that liars were bad innovators. They clung desperately to their alibis because elaborations led to inconsistency.

No one else would understand that this cowboy was now part of my Range, the only thing in my life that did not feel like a trap. Circling around my options, I came back to the same conclusion: I would not risk interference.

I decided to leave the shovel there, just in case. If he died, he would need to be protected from animals, at least for the time it would take to notify Lars and the North-West Mounted Police. He was lucky to have lasted this long without being bothered. His horse would be no match for a bear or pack of wolves. I might need to build him some sort of makeshift protection against rain clouds drifting in with the warming temperatures. Extra wood at the side of our shack could make a quick lean-to. I planned to take a few boards with me the next day and another blanket.

My path to the Range was oddly bountiful. With so many workers riding around town and needing to feed their horses, broken bales of hay lay scattered about, inviting me to stuff some into my sack for the horse. Rushing and feeding, rushing and feeding, my life was taken up caring for two men and a horse. I envisaged the cowboy awake so I could vent my frustration. Of all the millions of miles of bush in this forlorn country, how did it come to pass that you chose my one little private place to dither about meeting your Maker? Be done with it! One way or another, get on the road to somewhere—onto the next world or back where you came from! When I realised these ravings would easily have landed me in an asylum, I laughed maniacally just to hear what it sounded like.

As usual, I heard the horse rustling and huffing at my approach. Not until I was well into checking the cowboy's wound did I notice his eyes were open. I made no noise as I stared into those icy chips, mostly because my lungs struggled against the sensation of being suddenly filled with cement. My first thought was that these were the open eyes of a dead man, until he hoarsely asked for water. Wordlessly, I braced him to drink from my canteen. After a few silent moments, he gestured for me to come closer, as though, like Father, there was something important he wanted to impart, but he was too feeble to project his voice. I leaned forward and listened to a guttural wheeze.

—Go give that darn fool gun back to your daddy, you hopeless creature.

That was what he said. I wanted to slap him back into unconsciousness.

—You are the fool, sir, I told him. My father has never shot a gun in his life, and you do not look too adept in the art yourself at the moment. Evidently, someone better than you has shot your side off.

Surprisingly, he smiled, maybe more a wince, showing tobacco-stained teeth as he slipped back into unconsciousness. His horse nudged him with its nose, as though to rouse him, without response. I covered him back up, and had my practise session regardless.

Next time I returned to the Range, I saw from a distance the horse with its head low over the cowboy's face, listening to him. He had dragged himself over to a boulder where he had propped himself into a slump. When the horse saw me coming, it whinnied and threw its head up. The cowboy merely said he was thirsty. I indulged a moment of uncharitable irritation.

—I am not your nurse, I told him.

He seemed plunged into disorientation, as though suddenly unable to know me or where he was. I felt ungracious then.

—Nevertheless, I brought you water.

He tried to straighten himself out of his hunch, turn himself onto his side, and instead fell back weakly. If he were to eat or drink, I would have to help him. After taking a swig of water, he ate a couple of spoonfuls of porridge before waving me away. I gave the horse the carrot, which it wolfed down before stomping impatiently beside the invalid.

—You have some explaining to—

I had no chance to finish my sentence before the crack of a gun exploded behind me and a bullet whistled by, close to my head. Another bullet kicked up earth right next to my feet where the cowboy lay. Moving instinctively to confront the danger, I swung around in the direction of the shooter and pulled the trigger of my own rifle. There on the ridge, just above my tin cans, was a horse with a man. All I noticed about him was the black Mackintosh and the bowler hat falling off as he slumped over, teetered for several endless seconds in his saddle, and fell onto the ground with the sickening thud of a wet sack of flour.

Cautiously, I advanced toward the rumpled pile, my hammer cocked in case he was tricking me, and bent over to feel for a pulse. It was quite clear from the bullet that had blasted open the centre of his chest that he was stone cold dead.

GALVANIZED

For the longest time, neither the living cowboy nor I said a word. Even the horse that had until a few minutes ago carried a hale and hearty man on its back gaped at us dumbstruck. I tried to gauge whether it could comprehend the fact that it had just lost its mount for good. I certainly could not. After a time, the old cowboy croaked behind me,

—Well I'll be goddamned.

—Did you know he was coming? I demanded.

—I reckoned.

—He was tracking you?

—I reckon.

He laid his head back down on the ground and looked up at the sky, weakly laughing himself into a coughing fit.

—Girl, you got some powerful luck in you.

—Who have I killed?

—A Pinkerton. Snake's been on me for weeks.

—Did he shoot you from behind?

—Can't say as I remember.

—Well, I can tell from your wound that he did. It means you will live.

He laughed again.

—Ain't no way I'm going to live, one way or the other.

—There is no infection—

He just laughed and hissed and gurgled himself into insensibility until he passed out completely, all the excitement obviously too much for him. He would have loved to stay awake, I was sure, to enjoy the apparently hilarious ramifications of what I had done. That cowboy's ugliness went more than skin deep.

In a panic, I ran back to the village to see Lars, fully resolved to tell him I had accidentally shot a man with my new gun up in our back quarter. I was desperate to relieve my burden as the sole bearer of this information—sole except for that useless cowboy who did not count. Lars would commandeer my responsibility. He would shield me with his industrious self-importance. This protection was quite suddenly everything I wanted. As I burst through his door, he stood up, clearly alarmed by my sudden disruption.

—Lars, we simply must get a doctor here.

I surprised myself as much as I did him. He set down the box of fishing reels he was unpacking.

—Has he taken a turn?

—Not a turn, no, just more of the same. I fear he is losing ground.

—Day after tomorrow.

Having already forgotten what I had blurted, I could only nod my head to his answer as though I understood.

—Don't worry, Abigail, he said tenderly. You can count on me for anything you need.

I averted my eyes.

—I know that, Lars. Thank you.

I hung there, flushed, feeling his eyes roam over my face as though waiting for a sign of something more. Awkwardly, I nodded to him and bolted.

He truly was always there, lumbering in and out of his little store, noticing what everyone around him was doing. Why did that very constancy feel like a weight?

At home in the shack, listening to Father sleep, I paced the floor, my mind dashing out to the Range, the other invalid, the corpse, Father, and around again to the Range like a dog chasing its tail.

How could I have killed a man? My mind kept rejecting this horrible truth.

It then occurred to me: If I had killed a Pinkerton, I must be nursing an outlaw.

I had to go and find out who the man was. How else could I tell someone what I had done?

The cowboy's horse still stood watch over him only a few feet away. I had not thought to tether either animal. In retrospect, I was lucky that oversight had not compounded my problems. Riderless horses finding their way down to the village would have raised all sorts of alarms. Beyond the cowboy's horse, I espied the second horse foraging in a field, aloof but apparently unmotivated to run away.

Squatting down beside the dead man, I considered his red-ribbon bow tie and suspenders, odd fashion for such rough country. He marked himself as a foreigner in that outfit. I braced myself for the task of riffling through his pockets. It reminded me of the hordes of ghoulish scavengers that descended on the battlefield after the Battle of Waterloo to steal gold, jewellery, and teeth from the sea of prostrate bodies. To touch a dead stranger—the thought was abhorrent.

Gingerly, I tugged at the material of his trouser pockets until they pulled inside out with some coins. I took off his holster with two pistols and put them aside for later inspection. Then I unfastened his coat to check pockets, and was rewarded with a fairly large packet fastened with a clip.

As I pulled out each folded paper and smoothed it out, I noticed they were all maps. No identification. Why would a Pinkerton—a private lawman but a lawman just the same—have no identification? One would think any police organization that recently outstripped the size of the US army would have rules and regulations.

I thought I would be digging the hole for the cowboy, who woke up to watch me labour against rock to get the hole deep enough. Even if I did divulge my horrible deed, I still needed to cover him enough to protect him from the animals. He would have to be disinterred later and taken to wherever he came from. Unable to gouge out enough terrain to fit in the entire body, I had to throw myself into a frenzy of digging over and over again.

I must have been thoroughly demented, because the more I dug, the more resentment I felt toward Mr. Pinkerton, as I now thought of him. I did not know what else to call him. Did he think he could shoot me—especially in the back—and assume it would be that easy? If he thought I would not defend myself, he was a bloody coward. Surely he could have seen I held a rifle in my hands. With my trousers on, I looked like a man from behind, or at least a boy, meaning he could have assumed with even more confidence I would likely shoot back. And when I did, he gave no fight, just slumped off his horse, condemning me to endless quarrying, all the while consumed by my responsibility for his senseless fate. All he had to do was lie there. I asked for none of this.

At the peak of my outrage, the cowboy addressed me directly.

—I don't know your name, Girlie.

Sweating and furious, I refused to stop digging.

—Well, that is fair. Yours is a mystery to me, too.

—Shep January.

—Abigail Peacock.

—You got an accent.

—You are one to say. I am from England. I can tell you are from a Confederate state.

He looked hard at me for a moment.

—I am that. You got some questions for me. I'm ready to answer.

I went on digging.

—Where are you from?

—Ohio, originally. Then down through Missoura in the war. All over since then.

—What are you doing here?

—Runnin' from the law.

—Then you are an outlaw.

—Guess so.

—Have you robbed anything?

—Yep.

—Have you killed anyone?

—Yep.

—Then it is safe to say you are an outlaw.

—Guess so.

I stopped and turned to him.

—You either want me to know who you are or you do not. If you do not, get on your horse and get out of here. If you do, start talking, or the next time you see me I will have the police with me.

He could have shot me right there. Although my rifle was beside me on the ground, he was no doubt faster on the draw.

—I have a proposal for you.

—You can keep your stupid proposal to yourself. I have no interest in making any kind of deal with an outlaw.

We remained at a silent impasse as I conscripted his horse once more to move dead weight. I tied one end of the rope to the saddle and the other to the Pinkerton's belt. The horse followed my lead as we dragged the body into the shallow grave. I covered him over with all I had dug out. Anyone inclined to look closely could see the ground had been disturbed. Maybe after a rain or two it would look more natural.

In case the Pinkerton was a religious man, I had thought to bring Father's Bible and pronounced a few disingenuous words to approximate an appropriate burial. I even added in my own insincere apology at the end. Truth be told, my main regret was his imbecility to misjudge the situation so badly. If worst came to worst, I hoped a jury would see a clear case of self-defence, though I did not know how to prove it. The cowboy, hardly a credible witness, was the only one able to corroborate my story. I had already left myself in an equivocal position by not taking any action about the living man, short of giving him water over a couple of days and a bit of porridge when he was conscious.

When the doctor finally showed in the village, he concluded that Father did not have pneumonia, and that was why he failed to improve despite my most diligent nursing. I could barely believe it, but he thought Father had consumption.

This was a vile and infected place, but I would not have expected such a pernicious disease to bother existing where there were so few people to prey upon. The only treatment was rest, which he had been getting in extravagant doses. However, his age and frail constitution signified that his chances of pulling through were less than minimal. All we could do was keep him comfortable.

Now that I was cognizant of how dire things were with Father, I especially resented going up to the Range to take care of that outlaw. And yet, if I refused to go, how would he build up the strength to leave? I was feeding an additional man and two horses on the money I had left for just Father and myself. Not that the cowboy ate much. I could only look forward to him being sufficiently along on the road to recovery to soon get on his way with the animals. Then perhaps I would ask Lars to go to Kenora and report the Pinkerton's demise. As time went by, I saw my world filling up with guns and police and outlaws. Did this all happen because I bought a gun?

While the cowboy slept, I looked more carefully at the Pinkerton's pistols. Inlaid into the grips was a rich mother-of-pearl substance that flashed layers of lilac, mint green, and pale blue as I turned the guns back and forth in the light. It was a revelation to me that a gun maker would invest such artistry in a device meant for ruffians and built for violence. I pictured the Pinkerton giving self-conscious instructions to the gun maker about the subtle beauty he wanted, maybe even embarrassing himself, but not quite to the point of abandoning his request. Or maybe he happened upon them in a gun shop, where the merchant long anticipated the day a gunman would walk into his store in a wistful mood. In any case, Mr. Pinkerton must have treasured those guns.

The cowboy woke up for an hour, the longest time yet, and at first thought his memory was a happy dream until I confirmed there was indeed a basis in reality. Truly angry, I demanded an explanation for both of them so I could know the extent of the evil I had perpetrated. He wrapped his arms around his waist as he held in his wound, clearly ready to die content with that information, laughing until it hurt.

I got so frustrated that I shot my targets, fed him, and threatened not to come back. He merely stared me down with brutish eyes. If I had the stomach for it, I really would have left him to figure out how he was going to feed himself. He probably had some sort of food stashed in his saddlebags, which I had not touched.

The only positive sign in all this was that the cowboy's horse started wandering a bit more after the Pinkerton agent was dead. It was eerie, as though the horse knew danger was coming and felt responsible until a human provided safekeeping. Now it circumnavigated the Range area, even when I was there. I tied the horses together to ensure that the Pinkerton horse did not wander off too far from the field he had found for foraging. The cowboy's horse clearly had no mind to leave.

The lack of identification papers on the Pinkerton perplexed me. How did he expect to be monitored and ultimately claimed by his employer without some way of conveying who he was if he turned up dead? After setting aside the personal items I found on his body, I coaxed his horse to let me take off his saddle and the saddlebags. This horse was stout and light brown, a workhorse next to the other more regal one. It snorted through as much water as I offered, and competed with the cowboy's horse for the carrots I brought. I got the impression it was worn out from riding a long time.

I found one hundred American dollars in Pinkerton's saddlebag, an impressive amount of money next to the pittance Father and I lived on, and more than enough for a funeral, however rustic. I vowed to report what happened the moment I could leave Father for a couple of days without distressing him. If I waited too long for the cowboy to get out of here, I was petrified about being charged with harbouring a criminal, the least of my problems, I supposed, after having killed someone.

And I had yet to verify whether the cowboy was actually a criminal, since he was studiously vague, even under my most vigorous cross-examination. Come to think of it, how did I know Mr. Pinkerton really was a Pinkerton? He could merely have been dressed as one for some reason. In any case, if I were taken away from Father, he would surely perish, alone and terrified. The doctor thought Father would not last the summer as it was. I wished I had someone to talk to besides Lars. The cowboy could use the spoon by himself, but seemed in no hurry to leave.

When I felt I was going to burst, the gun channelled my turmoil straight into the target. I had two guns now, since I used Pinkerton's rifle for practise, too. His saddlebags were stuffed with enough ammunition to shoot anything crossing his path between here and the North Pole. Trailing days behind the cowboy, how could he have known where to go next? Evidently it was for good reason that Macdonald worried about Americans wandering back and forth across the border. Mr. Pinkerton was quite plainly unconcerned about boundaries.

He must have had a wife and children, or parents and siblings at least, who would have wanted to know if something had happened to him. Conceivably they might have made a pact about the number of days to lapse without checking in before someone would be spurred to look for him. That meant another Pinkerton could show up any time, even though the change in the cowboy's horse from restlessness to apparent serenity suggested not. I noticed he no longer pawed the ground or threw his head up like he used to.

To quiet my thoughts while falling asleep each night, I pictured my rifle braced securely in my arms shooting at the tin cans. In the stillness of this waking dream, I was in complete control. Even in reality, it was now an unusual occurrence for me to miss hitting a can. I had backed so far away from my shooting target that it appeared in my sights as a distant dot. The Pinkerton horse obliged me by letting me mount him while I shot. It was a new challenge to aim with so much bumping and moving as he walked. I read about a trap capable of sending clay birds into the air, sometimes a dozen at a time, requiring a frenzy of shooting. To do this while galloping on a horse would be a marvel. While I was on Pinkerton's horse that morning, I spied and shot at a hare as it flashed through the bushes. The shot went wide, but not by far.

Was I becoming bloody-minded in this harsh land? I could hardly bring to mind the young woman I used to be. Who was this person who killed a man, conjectured how best to report what she had done, and then put everything out of her mind to shoot her gun, however ineptly, at an animal? I was going to have to tell someone the truth.

Well enough to get on his horse and leave, the cowboy had instead decided to sprout roots. He watched me every day as I practised shooting. I threw him his food rather than fed it to him, so he knew he was unwelcome. I suspected he actually ate very little. He watched me without moving or uttering a word.

Pinkerton's rifle was much heavier than mine. I had been trying to work up my arm strength to steady the wobbling that happened when I aimed. There was an axle back at our shack that I rescued from a small wagon that fell apart. Father suggested we keep it in case it came in handy one day for trade. I pressed it toward my chest like a big dumbbell until my arms felt they might float away on their own. They were sore when I went to bed, and even stiffer when I woke up. Once I got out to the Range, they started to limber up and ultimately stood me in better stead for my target practise. I spent some of Pinkerton's money to keep us in provisions for a while, justifying it with the imperative that I would brook no interference with my ability to take care of Father.

I was sure the cowboy had something on his mind. He was up to something more than merely staring into space as he watched me. I could feel it. When I asked him point blank a couple of times if he wanted to say something—or at least tell me when he was planning to leave—he shook his head and waved his hand disdainfully. I pretended no one was there and went on with my practising, which, right or wrong, was the only thing that kept me adhered to my sanity.

Both the cowboy and his horse were waiting for me the next time I arrived at the Range and set up for practise. I had taken about five shots.

—I reckon I got some things to say, he called out.

—Then say them, I answered.

I fired my shot. Did he think I was going to drop everything because his lordship had finally found his tongue?

—I rode with the James Younger Gang. Maybe you heard of the Northfield First National Bank holdup in '76.

—How could I have heard of it? In 1876 I was thirteen years old in England.

He did not seem to know what to say to that, and I privately acknowledged that my resentment was perhaps uncalled for in this moment of conciliation. I took my rifle down from my shoulder and turned around to look at him.

—But the Jesse James Gang does sound vaguely familiar, I conceded.

I thought I saw the hint of a smile skitter across his cragged face.

—Jesse's face was too recognizable by then, he continued, especially when a man from the hardware store came into the bank just as everything was bustin' loose. It was raining so hard it was dark. We got to the horses best we could. Not all of us rode out. It was still raining by the time a posse of 500 men hunted us down.

He rambled out a list of names of men who were caught, injured, or killed.

—But somehow you got away?

He shrugged and nodded.

—Jesse and Frank got away, too, down through Iowa. Jim and Cole Younger are doin' life just over the border in Stillwater.

I knew this much to be true, anyway.

—After the war we started out. People cheered when we stopped a train. The newspapers called us rebels, but we was just soldiers livin' on after losin'. Maybe we couldn't win the war, but we could sure drag out those carpetbagger vultures come down to pick over bones.

—I do not hear anyone cheering you on now.

—The reward money went up. We robbed 'cuz that's what we did. When people started realizin' the gang was nothin' more than greedy, everyone turned into an enemy. I don't blame 'em. After Northfield, the gang was gutted.

—The gang did not end there, though, did it?

—Jesse tried to keep it goin'. All the men who were loyal to him from the war and after were either dead or in jail. New men had new reasons for bein' around him. We got good at war, then at holding up trains and banks. After Northfield, Jesse could end the gang or replace the fallen. Nobody came out of loyalty any more. They came for what they could get. Not from banks—from him. What they could get from him.

—Notoriety?

—Don't rightly know what that means.

—The chance to be famous.

—Well, if that means the chance to be undisciplined and disloyal and get a reward, then I guess that's so. Jesse was shot in the back by his own security guard three years ago. Frank surrendered six months later.

—I take it there is still a price on your head, then?

—I suspect so. You could make yourself famous, Girlie. You could go get those police you been talkin' about.

—I cannot figure out if you are simply enjoying your own story as you make it up, or if you really are a dangerous man.

—From where I sit, you're the one shootin' people dead.

He chuckled, then pulled the blanket up over his shoulder and sank back to sleep. I could not really argue with that.

Most days on my walk back to our miserable hut, I daydreamed about opening the door to find Father up and dressed, happily stirring a steaming pot of stew, chopping up onions and carrots, and chattering about building an extension onto the shack. In my mind he talked excitedly about ordering in a piano so we might have visitors, and suggested I speak to Lars about where we might purchase decent furniture. In these fantasies there was no Shep January, no Pinkerton, no horses.

I nearly unburdened myself to Father a thousand times, inevitably stopped by the knowledge that a new reason to fret would sap what little energy he had left. At least now he thought he had a solution in Lars. I had to concede, if only to myself, that I was alone in this world, too embedded in my current debacle to escape by any route but disaster. My longing to talk to someone reached excruciating proportions over the next two days as Father corroborated the doctor's prediction by lapsing into seeming unconsciousness. I could not go to the Range without assuring myself he would waken again. I had been so preoccupied with January these last days, I feared Father might have thought me less attentive.

When Father finally opened his eyes, he smiled at me, and I called out his name as though he had returned from the dead. Still groggy and stiff, he let me pull him up out of bed to his chair at the table, even roused himself to show some interest in eating and chatting. I doted on him fervently, aware with every spoonful I fed him that my days of having him to care for at all were cruelly numbered. Eventually he settled into his regular nap time, and I practically ran up to the Range. Breathless, I told January we had some decisions to make. I acknowledged to myself how ridiculous it was that I could unburden myself to an outlaw and not to a model citizen like Lars. I told him about Lars and Father, not because he would be the slightest bit sympathetic but rather because he needed to know I had other people monitoring my actions. I had more to do with my life besides take care of him. He simply had to get out of here.

—You are well enough to go now, I told him. I have yet to decide what to do about Mr. Pinkerton over there, but I can give you however many days' start you think you need.

—I won't be runnin' anymore.

—You are going to turn yourself in?

He laughed, and shook his head.

—These lungs is full of cancer, and no amount of runnin' is going to outrun that.

—You are dying, then.

—Yep.

—How long do you think you have?

—Few weeks, maybe a month. Two at most.

Deductions clambered over each other in my mind. What was the point of putting him in jail for the last few weeks of his life? If I left him until he died before I turned him in, how would I explain to the police that I left the Pinkerton agent so long? And what would it look like if I had two dead men buried out back? If Father expired, I would have my own private cemetery.

—You're a lousy shot, he said.

With him, a conversation never behaved like one. He could phase out and not respond to questions for hours. That all abruptly ended when he had something on his mind. I had to admit, I answered him rudely when he did this—quite out of character for me except that, in this rough land, one reverted alarmingly quickly to the brutal honesty of base human nature.

—You were the one on the ground with a bullet in you, January, and I am the one who saved you.

I was appalled at myself when I talked like this. I heard myself sound as though I were bragging about killing someone, which we both knew was a complete accident. Oddly, rather than laugh, he nodded.

—I seen that.

Was this a twisted compliment? I was tempted to tell him that if a fairy godmother offered to grant me one wish, I would choose a plan. Not a teaching plan from Lars, but a new idea, something daring, something to get me out of the troubles I saw mounting all around me like prison walls.

—I am ready to hear your proposal, I said.

He squinted as he watched me place my rifle on the ground and sit down to face him. I looked at him steady in the eye and waited. His nod was almost imperceptible.

—I want to stay here until I die, which won't be long, he said. I been on the move my whole life, and now I want to sit in one place until my time comes.

—None of us knows our date with our Maker, Mr. January. You could languish for months.

—That ain't what the doc said back home. I'm in the final stages, and I can tell you I feel it. What's more, I want it. I'm tired. I lived longer than I ever thought I would. Glory days is over, and I'm not up to new ones. You'd be takin' a risk on that, but I seen you take bigger ones right in front of me.

—Why do you want to die here?

—I don't care where I die, I just care about dyin' on my own, not helped out by any more like our visitor over there under your rocks.

—What difference does it make, if you are dying anyway?

—It's my legacy, Girlie. I want my people back home to know I went out on my own. I never went to jail. I was never taken down by Pinkerton, and I ain't never been crossed by my own.

—Why do you not go back and tell your own story? Or write a letter?

He laughed a bit and shook his head, more an expression of sadness than the usual ridicule.

—Too many places to visit. You see my condition. On my horse, I wouldn't make it far. If I did, there's all sorts I could bump into that would make fast work of my claim to a natural end.

—How is anyone going to know how you died if you do it way up here?

He took a deep breath, which set him to coughing. When the rattling and rasping settled down, he said,

—That's where you come in.

Seeing he had successfully ambushed me, he lay back on his bedroll again and closed his eyes. If I could have, I would have picked up my rifle and marched home. I could do no such thing now even if I tried, and he knew it. At length, he opened his eyes.

—You give me and my horse—I don't care what you do with the other horse—food and water 'til I'm gone. You bury me, just like you did that snake over there. Then, you take one of my pistols and one of his pistols, get on my horse, and ride back down south to meet up with Bill Cody's Wild West Show. You find Annie Oakley—she joined the show earlier in the year—and ask her where to find Shea Wyatt. I don't right know where he is now, but she will. When you track him down, you give him the guns and tell him I went out on my own and that you saw it with your own eyes. Tell him you buried me and the fool lawman on my tail. Wyatt can turn in the guns and protect you or defend you, whatever you need.

This was the plot of an adventure story I might have read about the wild west back when we were still in England and I was sane. More accurately, it was the fantasy of a desperate, dying man.

—You are quite the dreamer, Mr. January. I have a father here, and a life to carve out. There is a gold rush beginning in this region. All sorts of opportunities are arising for me. Even if I wanted to, I am not in a position to fly off on a wild goose chase, especially for such flimsy motivation as your manly pride.

—From what you've said to me, your father ain't likely to last as long as me.

—We do not know that for sure.

—The doctor told you he won't last another month.

I had forgotten I told him that.

—It don't matter when you leave. Wait as long as it takes for us both to be gone. Leave next year. Nothin' else is going to change in the meantime.

—It is a preposterous plan. I have no sense of direction or geography out here. I have no transportation, no money, no way of protecting myself. Women do not travel alone—

—I got the plan for that, too. I been laying here day after day workin' it all out. First, with the time I got left, I'll teach you how to shoot them guns right.

—You told me I was terrible.

—True enough, but you learn quick for teaching yourself. You ain't practising 'cause it's a hobby. I can tell some demon's drivin' you to shoot that gun. I can't make you a crack shot by the end of the summer, but I can show you how to practise. You'll have all the time you need after I'm gone.

I did not want to admit it, but a thrill raced through me at the thought of becoming a good shot. Apart from continuing along mulishly with what I was already doing, I had no sense for how to improve my aim or speed.

—What if you taught me, and I just packed up the guns into a box and sent them by post to Annie Oakley? She could give the guns to this Wyatt fellow.

He shook his head.

—Ain't sure enough. We stuck up stagecoaches and trains and took guns like these all the time. I know what can go wrong. Oakley might never get them, and even if she did, she might decide not to bother passin' them along to Wyatt. She's a powerful stubborn woman when she sets her mind against something. I need you to make it all happen. An' here's how you'll do it.

He pulled his saddlebags over with some difficulty and set them in front of me. Flipping up the leather flaps, he exposed packets of money bills stuffed inside.

—This here's thirty thousand American dollars I can't take with me. Yer friend over there could taste gettin' his hands on it. You do right by my dying wishes, and it's yours with my blessing. This, Abigail Girl, is the rest of your life.

CRUSHED

Anything over one hundred dollars simply did not compute in my penny-pinching mind. I was plagued with guilt about my luxury purchase of a gun. Adding a cow made me dizzy. Thirty thousand dollars was an unmitigated fortune. It would buy a grand house, a business, produce an income.

—That is stolen money, was all I could say.

—Yep, Yankee states run on stolen money. Go turn it in if you're so inclined. Find a charity. Don't make no difference to me.

—That money should be turned in to the authorities.

—Do what you want.

He rolled away from me on his bedroll and passed out. All this dastardly plotting had plainly enervated him.

I had always thought myself an upright, moral person. Without a moment's hesitation, I taught children never to take what did not belong to them. Even if they merely stumbled across property they knew was not theirs, they should be sure to give it to a responsible adult who would help them do the right thing. I never would have predicted I might be tempted, even for a moment, to rationalize an act of wrongdoing. And yet, rogue questions wormed into my mind.

What if the money started with a nefarious moneylender preying on some poor woman down south, forcing her to sell everything to hold onto her farm. He then took his money and boarded a train north, whereupon he was robbed in a Jesse James holdup. Despite the sense of poetic justice, the moneylender would be the offended party. Would true justice be served by returning the money to him? I sounded like Robin Hood and knew I was rationalizing. There were rights and wrongs, after all. If we let go of what we knew to be honourable in this new world, what would await? I knew it was right to turn in the money.

And yet, if January got the money by robbing trains, stagecoaches, and banks, to whom should the money be returned? January gave me something that was not his to give, and no one could definitively trace it to particular individuals. Whose money was it? Curiously, I thought of Riel. He said Rupert's Land was not a British king's to give away. God owned the land. If Riel thought the land was stolen from God, did Riel have the right to consider the territory now ownerless and open to be claimed by him? Original rental agreements with God did not prevent Indian lessees from fighting over square footage. In the end, Riel did not tell Canada to give Rupert's Land back to God. He and his Métis wanted more square footage in compensation. Did that mean this money that now belonged to no one in particular could be legitimized as reward money to send me on a journey?

Pinkerton must have been hired by someone who felt entitled to it, or maybe he wanted to steal it for himself. Maybe stealing from a thief amounted to something other than stealing, although an alternative word did not jump to mind at the moment. Did property unmoored from its original owners become newly claimable? Might this money now truly have been January's to give away?

That was as far as I was willing to suffer my own rampant speculation. I would tell January to take his money and go. There was nothing of value to be gained from accepting stolen money or standing up for the reputation of so thoroughly rotten a man.

I could tell by the way Lars talked to me about the school that he thought he had delivered the life I most wanted in this world, as though he had mined my most subterranean fantasy. He was partly right, too, since each morning I awoke convinced I was buried in a demented fairy tale. Two men had climbed inside my mind, a good one offering a life that seemed to follow me wherever I went, the bad one a life I could never invent.

After twenty-two years, I found myself in a frenzy of doubt about who I was and what I wanted. Not so long ago I was a sensible girl, devoted to her mother, dedicated to moulding young minds and producing respectable members of society. Now I was a wild woman with a gun and a taste for blood and adventure. I did not want to *talk* anymore; I wanted to *do*, even if I was unsure of what was right or wrong at the moment. What an imbecile I was. I wanted to ride on my horse and shoot at something—a can, a boulder, the target itself was immaterial to me. This could not be my right mind. I pictured myself hopping on January's horse and racing off at breakneck speed into the sunset. I had no idea what a life of adventure even meant beyond shooting at my silly target range.

If I continued to appear committed to teaching at the school, I might deflect Lars from dissecting the reasons I would offer to warrant quitting. Mornings were my favourite time, when Father fell back to sleep, freeing me to hurry up to the Range in time to practise my shooting. By the time the Swedes returned from their work in the mines, presented themselves with their stubby pencils and hopeful smiles, I greeted them as their dependable schoolmistress eager to conduct them through their ABCs. All the while, Mother Goose pined to stick one webbed foot out the back window. Then I went home to cook, wash, and take care of Father.

Later, when Lars dropped by, I was alarmed by how easily he presumed to enter now without knocking, supposedly because Father was so much worse and should not be disturbed if sleeping, even if it meant delaying dinner. Already Lars and I were growing into new roles, his as the village mayor and mine as the schoolmistress. Soon the Finns and Swedes would see us as mother and father to their education. Tongues would wag about the way we worked as a team, how similar we were, and how perfect we were for each other. One day he would slip into referring to me as Mother.

For the first time, Lars paid me Father's stipend directly because I was doing his job. Father was delusional to think he might have supported us on this amount, especially now that the small savings we brought with us was spent. I kept detailed notes of all finances in a small notebook that I stowed under my pillow. One section logged Pinkerton's money, which I had to dip into, but only in an amount justifiable as payment for digging his grave. Lars probably assumed Father had a small legacy stuffed under the mattress.

It was uncanny how the falling away of financial privation changed one's dreams! January's offer enticed me like forbidden fruit. Or, perhaps until now, what I wanted from life was shaped by my own circumscribed image of what I thought practical or possible. Just a glimpse of a life without the usual limits made me feel strangely free of what I always assumed was my lot. Even without his fortune, here was a new pursuit I never considered.

Once not so very long before, I was willing to do anything to protect Father. Now I knew that there was nothing I could do in the long run to achieve that end. He would be mortified by my temptations now. And Lars, who granted my every wish as a well-supplied and appreciated teacher, would be devastated to know what tempted me. He created dreams for his fledgling citizens, and proved himself worthy of followers.

As ungrateful and shallow as I incontestably was, I did not want to invest my life in a cabin where I lived out my days one thin board away from unending muck and trees and snow and rain. I wanted the excitement of a city, of ideas, of fashion and skill. I did not want to contribute to others; I wanted to act for myself. I wanted the kind of life that befitted an epic New World. I wanted to know how to shoot and ride and explore. Here, January came—from Heaven or Hell, I did not know—prepared to grant me a fateful wish.

I gave Lars a list of books, along with a request for newspapers from beyond Winnipeg and Lakehead—maybe Toronto, Chicago, or Minneapolis—officially to help our students expand their understandings of the world around them. All of that was true. He did not need to know I was also feeding an idle curiosity regarding the whereabouts of Bill Cody's Wild West Show. Even with no intention of accepting January's blood money, there was no mischief in a little harmless research.

The world was shrinking for everyone around me—Riel, January, Pinkerton, the Younger brothers, even Father—but I was flush with new possibilities. I hurried up to the Range for my first lesson with January. He was apparently still willing to teach me despite my refusal to commit to his journey. While Father was alive, I would not even consider his demise, no matter what a doctor said; doctors were wrong more frequently than people realised.

The only thing I had fully decided to do was deprive January of the satisfaction of knowing just how much his proposal of the journey had crept under my skin. Most days I lived in a perpetual outrage at him, first for crashing into my life, then for roping me into his puerile wish for a legacy. Or trying to. I focused on the disruption he had brought in getting himself shot on my Range, the danger his presence had caused me with the Pinkerton hot on his trail, and the horrible predicament he had led me into now that I had killed someone.

I scowled at him, scoffed at his plans, and yet brooded over the chance he might see through the bluster of my deep desperation to go. I forbore admitting even to myself the secret wells of excitement that bubbled up inside me. I would never let him know he had a genius for feeding me exactly what I wanted.

January shrugged at all my concerns and conditions.

—There's no particular hurry, 'cepting we better get started before I run out of time. That'd leave you to makin' a fool of yourself every time you pick up a gun for the rest of your life.

He pointed his rifle at the treetop he intended to shoot, clipped the tufted branch right off the tree, and looked at me as though I was supposed to have learned something.

—Now you do it, he said.

—I am going to need more guidance than that.

—There ain't no more guidance comin'. Look at the lay of the land like a shooter. Expect what can move to move; expect what can't move to stay still.

—I cannot learn just by watching you.

—How the hell else are you going to learn?

—Tell me things, how to change my stance or hold the gun or how to aim. I know *you* can shoot. Show me how *I* can!

—This is how, he yelled, and fired at a hawk over us. It fell with a thud a few yards away.

—Now look what you have done. I am not cleaning that. Can you even eat a hawk? All I learned there is that *you* can shoot, which does not help *me*.

I was not proud of it, but I ran all the way home, determined never to go back. If teaching were that easy, all I had to do was sit at a desk all day reading and writing. How would any of my students learn from watching me do what I did? Father asked me what I was thinking about so seriously as I fed him, which jolted me into a recognition of how intense I had become. I lied, of course, telling him I was figuring out where we would put the cow and how I might make cheese, which made him smile. I could actually do it now with Pinkerton's money.

—People spend their lives learning to make cheese, Abby, he rasped. There is a skill to it.

—Well, no one is born with such knowledge. How am I supposed to learn it on my own?

He looked at me quizzically, since I had raised my voice.

—I am sorry, Father. You are right. It is best to think of the cow as a provider of milk, which will be helpful in its own right.

Sleep eluded me as my mind kept repeating, over and over, what January did. I recalled his careless aim, as though his gun were doing the thinking for him without the need for him to even pay attention. How did he do that and still pick a bird right out of the air? He needed merely to point at something, and an invisible ray of some sort shot out ahead of the bullet to guide it. He was no more a teacher than I was a shooter, but if I missed the chance to learn from him, I would never forgive myself.

I tried to stay away, even managed to skip a day by pacing the cabin while Father slept. For a few hours I read the newspaper until the Swedes finally arrived after their day in the mine. On the morning of the second day, I could hear the horse sense my approach, as always. I smelled no fire until I crested the boulders to the Range. I looked for bones from the dead hawk but saw nothing. Straight away, he picked up his rifle and heaved it over to me.

—1878 Parker Brothers sixteen-gauge double-barrelled, breech-loading shotgun with external hammers, he said.

It wobbled as I strained to keep it braced against my shoulder.

—You better double those repetitions on the weight-liftin', he grunted.

Instead of cans on my target shelf, he placed a pebble there.

—I can barely see it, no less hit it.

—Then you need to figure out a new way of lookin'. In the west there's a long way to see.

We were now locked in a contest to see who might appear the more indifferent. He was evidently as invested as I was in pretending he cared less one way or another whether I went.

My arms ached so badly, I awoke in the mornings wanting to cry. I could barely lift the spoon for Father's porridge, yet by the time I rinsed the dishes and moved Father from his bed to a chair in the sunshine for a little while, my arms proved serviceable once more. It was an odd sensation to have arms that felt like they were going to break one day, and yet soon be able to lift more than ever. It certainly changed what one thought a reasonable demand of the body.

I was tucking Father in for the night when he signalled for me to come close so he could whisper something into my ear.

—I often wonder where you go while I am asleep.

—I have bought a rifle, Father, from Lars. I practise with it each day at a shooting range that I built up behind the village.

At first I suspected he had misunderstood, with his face so still and eyes unmoving, his hands lying folded in front of him. For a moment I thought he had expired right there in front of me. I expected consternation, worry at least, even disapproval. Then he coughed.

—I have heard those gunshots off in the distance, he said torpidly. I hope you become a very good shot.

I toyed for a moment with confessing the fantastical plan that captivated me. I hugged him, took his hand, and, when he said nothing more, determined I would let him lie as peacefully as he could within the small ambit that had become his world.

I learned how to ride sidesaddle, a peculiar thing for January to show me since he thought it a "damned idiotic" way to ride a horse—it threw off the centre of gravity, leaving one less anchored as a rider. He thought horses actually laughed at women who rode this way. While I should ride astride like a man for travelling, women were supposed to ride sidesaddle, and I should know how to ride like Annie Oakley.

A sidesaddle that was specifically designed to support riding tricks had a hook on it you could use to brace yourself. I should get one of these saddles as soon as I found a saddle shop along my journey. The rougher women shooters rode "regular," as January termed it, but Annie Oakley had big opinions about how women should ride and shoot. She was bullheaded about being ladylike, so I should track her for a while to get to know her slowly, study her for my best approach. If she took a dislike to me, she would never help me no matter what I did, and she was most likely to take a dislike to a woman shooter.

Oakley and her husband were paranoid about her reputation as a lady because they saw the show world as degenerate. She would not want anything to do with me unless I presented myself as above the riff-raff of bad-talking women shooters and men who could hardly stand up from drink an hour after the show. I assured January I was not likely to be mistaken for a bad-talking performer.

He thought I needed to get a job with the troupe so I could spend some time figuring out how to befriend her. I might need to stay with the show for a while to find Wyatt, since he was not likely to be with them all the time. I also needed a strategy for handling the journalists. January said they were vermin with a special ability to sniff out stories about outlaws. If they discovered I had the guns of a Pinkerton and a James-Younger Gang rider, they would badger me right out of my mind. The trick to tracking people was creating smokescreens to avoid being obvious about why you asked about anyone in particular. I would never have been able to figure this out on my own.

I was so sore, I could sit down only gingerly. He was right that sidesaddle was a precarious way to ride. I could only presume the same kind of mind that came up with that style also had a hand in designing corsets and high-heeled shoes.

January said his horse was named Abe, after President Lincoln.

—That is quite a compliment to your man of freedom, I told him.

—It ain't no compliment.

—Why not?

—I was a Confederate soldier.

—Then why did you name your horse after a Union president?

—So I could holler at him for the rest of my days.

Why was that horse so loyal to him? After being cussed at so long, why did he not take his opportunity to escape when January was sprawled listless on the ground? I was connected to him simply because he contained in his head the information I wanted to transfer to mine. The horse stood a good chance of finding food and kindness from someone else by escaping and offering himself up to another owner.

I speculated how Abe might take to me if I ever actually decided to become his rider. The logistics of this trip were impossible: the harsh terrain, my inexperience on a horse, no less as a wild-west rider. I really had no intention of ever doing it, but out of my own curiosity I asked January what I should do with Pinkerton's horse.

—Take him with you.

—That would be an awful lot to manage, trying to control and feed two horses.

—Pinkerton's horse will follow Abe, and Abe knows what to do.

—Why is Abe so well behaved?

—He knows what it's like to run for his life. I kept him alive. He knows it.

—You are also the one who put him in danger.

—He don't know that.

—He would surely figure out I have no idea what I am doing.

—It ain't that complicated, Girlie. You show him you're boss 'cause you won't take no for an answer. Then, you take the simplest route from where you come from to where you're going. Abe don't know where you're goin'.

—What if somebody figures out that I have a Pinkerton's horse?

—Nobody's goin' to know that just from lookin' at him. If somebody accuses you of stealin' a horse, say you're on your way to return the horse and tell on me killin' a Pinkerton.

—But that changes the entire story. Then I would have to explain how you died. And then people would want to know what happened to your stolen gang money and where your body was, which would make me look even more suspicious. Do you think that Pinkerton knew you had all that money with you?

He looked at me as he rolled tobacco into his paper. When he lit it, he coughed out a dry laugh.

—Already thinkin' 'bout how you're goin' to protect yer money, are ya?

—I would never keep the money. I have every intention of giving back what you stole.

He was an infuriating man.

I caught Father trying to hide the fact that his lungs were bleeding. If not so fixated on the Range and the school, maybe I would have apperceived how much his condition had worsened. The doctor came through town again and left with the conviction Father had deteriorated to the point that he could go at any time. I was aghast it could be so soon. Some people lived for quite a while with consumption. I had read newspaper stories of patients told they had only months to live, and yet they survived for years, even decades.

On my better days I held out hope the doctor was wrong. Maybe another doctor would diagnose something else. Many conditions and diseases manifested in a horrible cough and general lassitude. This doctor's diagnosis was based on simple examination without corroborating tests. On these days I saw Father so clearly in my mind's eye with the morning sun behind him and a mug of tea in his hand. On days when I was not so confident, I feared he would expire before me by minute's end.

I avoided school for the next few days, telling Lars I had to tend to Father in his turn for the worse. I did, however, continue to sneak up to the Range each morning to receive my lesson. The regularity with which Father slept at that time allowed me to convince myself I was not abandoning him for my own selfish pursuits, even though that was exactly what I was doing and did not seem about to stop.

I always presumed a woman's softer touch encouraged the flowering of inquisitive minds. I never questioned the efficacy of constant talk and explanation in massaging growth, the way ants coaxed open the bloom of a many-layered peony. January simply grunted if I missed a target. I noticed but would never admit to him that my reaction was to sharpen my skill instantly.

I saw nothing in the newspapers about Bill Cody's Wild West Show. I deliberated about why that was, since January insisted it was on tour. Perhaps it was carried only as local news in the city where it was next bound. I was at a loss. If I did not know where it was or where it was bound, I had no idea what paper to try to order. What reason would I give Lars for requesting newspapers from random cities all over the northeast US?

All was talk about Riel's defeat at Batoche. Father was right that no amount of Gabriel Dumont's tactical genius as Riel's military general could change the long-term odds of staving off an army that outnumbered his men many times over and had the benefit of unending supplies of ammunition. Now processions of soldiers marched home carrying grotesque effigies of Riel dangling from mock gallows. I honed in on the story of the Northcote Ferry. Dumont conducted a naval battle in a prairie surrounded by a million square miles of land. He had a farm outside Batoche and ran a ferry service across the Saskatchewan River. General Middleton decided to send some of his men to sneak down the river on the ferry from the south to line up with the west side of Batoche, while he could attack from the east on horseback with the troops.

The coming battle grew personal for Dumont when he discovered that, on their way down the river, the thirty soldiers aboard the Northcote had first stopped at Dumont's homestead. While he might not have pinpointed that the decks of the Northcote were reinforced by beams, plywood, and grain from his own newly non-existent barn, nor that it was his mattresses that buffered the windows, he did mark his billiard table and his wife's washing machine strapped to the deck as defensive armaments. The Northcote's trip down the river proceeded faster than expected, and Dumont was waiting for them with more ferocious resistance than they expected.

Dumont's men retrieved the cable normally used to pull the ferry along, and instead stretched it across the river so the boat would become trapped by it. The cable was not lowered fast enough. Instead of stopping the steamboat, the cable sheared off everything affixed to the deck, including the smokestacks and whistle. The distraction deteriorated into comedy as the boatload of helpless Canadian soldiers drifted aimlessly another four kilometres down the river, the Métis laughing uproariously from both banks as they continued to take potshots.

Dumont's army back at Batoche was vastly outnumbered, though, and, after three days of fighting, ultimately overrun. He must have known the inevitable result. By the time their white flags were tendered and the miserable little arsenal surrendered, the warriors had been reduced to jamming their guns with pebbles for ammunition.

When Lars related stories of these battles, he emphasized the certitude of the rebels' demise. He concentrated on the numbers of soldiers whose dedication won the day, despite their lack of military experience. He extolled the determination of Macdonald, who jumped into action when it was needed, and in enough time to ensure a swift victory. He celebrated the engineering prowess of Van Horne in cobbling together the railroad so it might become iconic as the achievement of Canada, not only as a nation sea to sea, but as a demonstration of the genius to make it work. When Father was awake during any of these discussions, he offered weak exhortations in defence of Queen and Country. Sometimes I deduced he had forgotten that he was not back in England worrying about the Scots.

In Dumont, I detected a man of action, who used whatever he had at hand to execute what was important to him. His demise was not inevitable. Had he hit hard and fast in every way he wanted, he might have eclipsed Middleton's arrival with enough time in hand and nuisance value to Macdonald to win concessions. It was Riel who hobbled him, and it was Dumont who let him. Had Dumont insisted on his action plan from the beginning, told Riel to mind his own business on the military front, he might well have wound up behind a treaty table rather than a white flag.

Rumour had it that during the wait for Middleton to arrive at Batoche, Riel was orchestrating votes in his Provisional Government to rename the days of the week—Monday to Christ Aurore, Tuesday to Vierge Aurore, Wednesday to Joseph Aube, Thursday to Dieu Aurore, and on it went. Men subjected to this bizarre litany were likely attuned to the tremor under thousands of marching boots advancing on them from not so far away. The more impossible their situation, the more Riel believed God would work a miracle to save them. A miracle required an impossible situation, and he was intent on delivering that.

After the surrender, Dumont searched for Riel for days, wanting to take him into another exile over the American border. Riel remained elusive until he turned himself in. When Middleton took Riel into custody, Major Young was ordered that, should any attempt at rescue be mounted, he was to shoot Riel first and fight off the attackers second. Apparently, such an attempt never materialized. Dumont demonstrated the good judgment of saving himself.

Now that Riel was in custody, he was a fascination to all kinds of people. Apparently he differed from his fellow Catholics in his conviction that the pope could not possibly be infallible. He pointed out that many popes had made obvious and extravagant mistakes, a remarkably rational observation for a zealot. That he was devout, no one questioned, but he struck a new direction when he said the faithful were the holy ones who should become more directly involved in steering the course of the church's decision-making. He charged that the priests used the pope's infallibility for their own power. At present, Québec was ruled by Rome, and Riel did not think foreigners should rule his countrymen.

I remained torn between the crazy life made possible by the dying man of action back at my Range, and the sensible one Lars was building here. He planned to expand his store into a hotel along the shoreline of Wabigoon Lake, where the train track ran. So much freight was funnelled through Wabigoon every day that we were growing accustomed to new men appearing out of nowhere, unloading, and getting back in their boats for more. People from all over who brought in mining equipment traded rumours of a lumber mill that might be built farther west.

A simple wooden church was going up, and the Swedes had their hearts set on starting a newspaper. One of the first editorials they intended to write was about the present storage site for the mines' dynamite. There was a pile outside town that was close enough to damage property if lightning were to strike. Soon the streets would be surveyed. Lars was right that a hotel would meet the needs of those who had not yet built their own proper cooking facilities. I shuddered to think he might have me in mind for his kitchen in the morning and schoolroom in the afternoon.

I functioned mostly as a nurse, replacing compresses on Father's forehead until he wakened in need of my gentle thumping of his back to dislodge the building mucous that threatened to drown him. Time stood still in our little shack of illness, and I thought about nurses who worked like this hour after hour and day after day. In the American Civil War they probably knew some of the men they tended. That would be horrible. I thought of them as I drowned in the long seconds between Father's coughing fits when he panted for the air that eluded him.

I saw in the paper what Lars was talking about. It reported that 779 Métis signed the petition demanding recognition of their title to the land. Of them, 568 did not qualify because they had received their land and scrips in Manitoba, were from the United States, or were squatters who were not Métis at all. Only 193 were eligible for scrip. Plainly, their resistance was about something more than land.

The expectation that a guilty verdict in Riel's trial was a foregone conclusion did not slake people's appetite for details. The importation of prosecution lawyers from Toronto and Québec prompted some to ask why the perfectly capable hundred or so lawyers already available in the northwest were bypassed. Some said this trial was actually about the murder of Tom Scott fifteen years ago. Riel, conceivably because he would not enter a guilty plea for the lower charge of treason-felony, was the only one charged with high treason, a charge for which a guilty verdict required death. He wanted the trial to be held in Québec, and to discuss the two rebellions as one, but apparently the law said jurisdiction was in the northwest.

Riel's trial was set down in Regina, the new target of all eyes and ears. Dumont was rumoured to be planning an attack on the army of North-West Police officers stationed around the courthouse. Some predicted he would wait until Riel was found guilty and transferred to a jail that might be penetrated at night by stealth, with assistance from the many Riel sympathizers. While Dumont inspired dread in those charged with foiling his efforts, I could not see this brilliant tactician following through with a suicide run.

Newspaper headlines metamorphosed from war stories like "A Prisoner's Tale" and "Our Noble Defenders" into the permutations of court: "Selection of the Jury and Opening of the Case," "Mr. Osler's Address for the Prosecution," "A Number of Witnesses Examined—Riel's Conduct at Duck Lake and Batoche," "Close of the Case for the Prosecution Yesterday," then "Riel Desires to Supplement Counsel's Efforts," "General Middleton in the Witness Box," and now "Dependence Placed on the Plea of Insanity," "Evidence from the Doctors and the Priests," and "The Opinions of the Lunacy Experts—Riel Believes in His Own Sanity."

The articles pointed out that through most of the prosecution's case, Riel was visibly agitated until he erupted on the second day with the information that he was unhappy with his counsel. While the prosecution argued Riel knew what he was doing, his own counsel offered a plea of insanity. Riel insisted on the dignity accorded an intelligent being. A five-minute recess was called so defendant and counsel could come to some sort of agreement, which conspicuously did not hold. Once the trial resumed, Riel pleaded once more to speak for himself, thereby compromising the argument of his defence. His counsel began with the argument that the rebellion was rationally justified because the federal government ignored the legitimate complaints of the Métis, and then turned back on itself to claim that, even though the rebellion was justified, Riel was insane.

Witnesses for the defence were an odd assortment of political analysts and lunacy doctors who countered eyewitness accounts from police and others who had the chance to interact with Riel and found him quite lucid. On the face of it, Riel was only insane when he spoke about politics and religion, which would place him in good company with many I knew back in England. Could you be mad only on certain topics? Some said one is insane on the basis of not knowing right from wrong. These lunacy doctors claimed one could be well aware of legal wrongdoing and still go ahead and act in an insane way because of a disease of the mind.

Two of the doctors diagnosed him with megalomania, evidenced by his ambition to make a new religion and nation. Perhaps a hundred years later doctors would have discovered how to define insanity definitively, whether it is a global disease of the entire brain, a disease that hides in certain topics, or one that can come and go based on situation, even whether it can come and go completely.

I was churned up about Riel largely because each headline forecasted impending doom: "The Prisoner Makes a Speech to the Jury," "He Appreciates the Double Line of Defence," "The Case to Go to the Jury To-Day—An Early Conclusion Expected." It was not as though I wanted him exonerated. There were sixty-seven whites killed and 110 wounded, with sixty-one half-breeds killed and eighty-two wounded, declared the *Manitoba Daily Free Press*. These were real husbands, sons, fiancés, uncles, friends, lovers, leaders, warriors, and hunters whose lost lives cried out to the living to make sense of what happened.

Incredibly, there was no end to Riel's demands. He wanted two million acres earmarked as an endowment for the building and maintenance of schools, hospitals, and orphanages. This he saw as a down payment for the eventual value of a new Northwest Territories nation. His calculation was based on a market value of forty cents an acre for the entire area, to be divided between the Indians and Métis at the rate of twenty-five cents to the Métis and fifteen cents to the Indians. Further, he wanted one hundred thousand dollars for himself, which he considered the value of the land he had to give up back in 1869, when he was banished for his role in the insurrection in Manitoba. Although, he insinuated that he might settle for thirty-five thousand dollars.

It must have been past midnight. I had been sitting in the dark beside Father's bed for hours, listening to him struggle to breathe. Somewhere in the recesses of my soul, I knew this was his last night on this earth. I lit a lamp with the flame low as my grief expanded in my mind to crowd out all else. I was losing the only person in the entire world I loved. On the strike of an hour, maybe the next one or the one after that, I would be completely alone.

I thought of Mother as I watched him lying on his deathbed.

He must have done the audit she talked about. No doubt he concluded himself a foolish man, saved once by a prudent wife but later encouraged into self-destruction by a reckless daughter. What inventory would I take when it came my turn? Would I thank my lucky stars that level-headedness prevailed, and I eked out a stable existence, perhaps not with a man I loved but one I grew to respect? Perhaps I would rue that decision as a coward's way of avoiding the adventure that had spectacularly if incomprehensibly been offered to me on a platter. Mother regretted her decision to stay, and Father regretted his to go. There was obviously no easy answer to discern from their decisions.

Sitting with Father, holding his hand as he struggled, made me think about the occasions in my life when I was finely tuned to the breaths I took, the sounds I heard, the textures and colours that fed my touch and vision. I was most alive in moments of calm, when I knew what I wanted. I had to admit my convictions, whether I wanted them to be true or not. As I stared down death, it was time to face my own facts.

I did not want to teach.

I did not want Lars.

I did not want to stay here.

I wanted someone to help me turn in the guns and stay out of jail.

Most of all, I wanted to shoot. I wanted to learn all I could from January, and then I wanted to seek out others who could teach me more.

I was on the brink of my own destiny, beholden to no one, soon to be my own lonely mistress. Father chose what he would do with his life. I would decide what to do with mine.

I decided to tell no one—especially not that infuriating January—but I would go on his benighted journey. Annie Oakley would be my beacon, and shooting my salvation. That is what I wanted to do. That was what would make my life worth living.

Father rallied at the end, and the last words he said were "I have always loved you." I watched helplessly as he sank for the last time into unconsciousness, with me aching to pull him back, his breathing oddly regular until the moment it simply stopped, painless from what I could tell. Living had become such a trial for him, I had forgotten what his face looked like in relaxed repose.

At every turn now, Lars materialized beside me. He arranged for a burial in our makeshift cemetery on the far side of what we had come to call a mission. We called it that to avoid calling it what it was: a crude set of benches with no mysticism to elevate it. The absence of a missionary here until the church was completed created a welcome gap for Lars as the substitute minister to perform the service with the same Bible I used to bury the Pinkerton. Lars spoke in confidential tones to me, intimate in his conveyance of understanding. He was as inevitable and ubiquitous as mosquitoes in summer. Did he assume that I was too delicate to read at my father's funeral? We buried Father two days later, after I had the chance to prepare him.

After the funeral, I retreated to the shack while Lars busied himself with what I was only too aware was the grinding effort of digging a grave. Word of my unsociability proved contagious, thankfully warning away well-wishers from my door. I longed for a cocoon. When late in the day I hauled myself up to the Range, January was sitting quietly and smoking, the food I left the day before untouched.

—You do not have much of an appetite, I said as I reached him.

He shrugged.

—I just buried my father.

Maybe I expected a sympathetic grunt, maybe a wise word from someone staring into the same abyss, some shred of companionship.

—Better get to work, then, he said, and handed me one of the pistols from his holster. He remained seated, and I had the impression he was too weak to get up. Another perishing man in my life.

My instinct to recoil at his insensitivity passed remarkably quickly. What else was he to do? Should I have expected from him a sad reverie about death? Whatever approximation of a deal we had was business, and even on that basis any presumption by him to give consolation would have been met with my admonition to mind his own business.

Up to now we had practiced shooting with a rifle, but if I had to defend myself I had better be able to reach for a pistol faster than a hummingbird's flap. The psychology of the interaction was as important as the weaponry, sometimes more, and my best defence was offence. January advocated I should dress like a man to avoid attention. From a distance a rider in a jacket, pants, and wide-brimmed hat might be anyone so long as I emitted the scent of knowing what I was doing and where I was going. Be a skunk, he told me. Repel the kind of men who picked on those who appeared weak.

Confronted by a single rider, I should have my pistol cocked from early in the approach, and be prepared to use it at the first sign of hostility. Waiting for a second sign could come at the price of my life. While the more concerning instance was a situation wherein I had to handle more than one man, groups conglomerated mostly around towns and cities and were easily frightened by anyone appearing crazed.

I drank in everything he told me, especially now that I knew my life would depend on his instruction. He could not have known the extent of my commitment. I changed nothing about my interaction with him. He did not ask what I would do once he was gone, and I silently pledged to myself every day that I would make sure he died never knowing the answer to that question.

He taught me that there was a markedly different feel to shooting a pistol compared to a rifle mounted at the shoulder. I could counter any kick to the shoulder by leaning into the gun with the full weight of my body, while a pistol at waist level forced a recalibrated aim and more arm strength. The first several shots that flew wild roused me to compensate by lifting my arm to eye level where I could align a dependable fix on my mark. January insisted I practise lower down for times when I might not get the chance to line up my target. Regardless of my skill level, the best insurance on an intractable shot was to shoot as many times as there were bullets in the gun.

When the session was over, he said,

—For the record, I won't thank you for no Bible readin'. Just get me deep enough in the ground that no animal gets me. If you ever need to prove my bones are here, you'll be able to find them.

I nodded and left.

It was October already. With Father gone, I felt no urgency to make a stew or even a bed. All that remained was an empty shack. I lost my will to do anything but shoot. Over those past weeks, one shooting lesson blended into the next, and even January disappeared from my plane of awareness, except that on some level I remarked that he gradually spent more and more time asleep. Whenever he awoke even for a few minutes, he told me something new to do, which I practised until he wakened again, maybe sometime that day or the next or the next. If he did not die of cancer, he would die of starvation. He hardly ate anything.

When I was not shooting at the Range, I was teaching the Swedes, not inspired teaching that opened eyes to new worlds but rather the refuge of endless repetition. Lucky for me they were so tired after a day of physical toil, they did not seem to mind the deadening rewriting of words or the endless rehearsal of their pronunciation. They were a comforting choir to me because their voices made no demands. I saved all the newspapers from Riel's trial for them to read out loud to each other. One day they could summarize the arguments on their own, even conduct mock debates to figure out for themselves what to make of it all.

I went up to the Range and found Shep January dead. It took me the rest of the day and the morning of the next to bury him. I chose a spot on the other side of the Range so nobody could get him mixed up with Pinkerton. I was convinced Abe knew what I was doing since he showed no distress as I covered January up in the rocky earth. When I clucked the low noise January taught me, Abe came immediately. I gave him an apple and also rewarded Pinkerton's horse, who sure enough followed Abe without hesitation. I decided to call the horse Pinkerton, since the man had owned it and the horse needed a name.

I stayed and taught for the rest of the week so that I could put two days of travelling behind me over the weekend before Lars determined I was gone. I left a note for him in the shack elucidating I could not bear to live where I had so many memories of Father. In truth, my one regret in leaving here was the trove of memories it delivered about his last two years. This was his life's adventure; it was awful, but it was now his resting place. Part of me would always feel a bit of home here.

Wretched as it was of me to abandon Lars like this, I did not want him getting any pointless ideas about talking me out of leaving. He would be inclined to impress upon me with great patience that it made no sense to decide anything in the midst of my grief over this winter. The prudent course was to wait and see how I felt in the spring. Any counter-argument I pressed would sound pathetic or impulsive. All winter he would drop by with things to give me—a turnip here, a pot there, my newspaper perhaps every day. There would be a never-ending supply of school business to discuss—students' progress, the details that would lead us to thinking through his plans to expand. Then, one day, he would deliver his logical proposal that we join forces instead of continue as two lone wolves, and I would have no more excuses to keep him or the life he offered at a distance. I had no way of telling him I was obsessed with the ludicrous thought of riding out of town with my horses and guns and the freedom to lay my head down in territory as yet unknown to me.

LAUNCHED

My first observation about life on a horse was that it interfered with jotting things down in my logbook. I allotted several pages up front to recording what I did with my various sources of income, my teaching money, Pinkerton's money, and January's money. In another section, I dedicated space to various and sundry lists. I wanted to remember whether the sun shone, if there was snow, how cold I guessed it to be, what animals I scared out of the bush as we plodded west. I doubted January ever felt the need to tack details onto a mental map in the hope of pinning life into place. I needed to see the overall trajectory, where I went and how I arrived there. I knew it was impossible. How could I blaze a tree to find my way back to Father's death, identify a landmark for January's sudden appearance in my life, or even find directions for who I was back in England? Still, I wanted to record the march of details on this journey, the colours and textures I encountered along the way.

There was no justification for my adventure other than informing the authorities what I did to the Pinkerton. While it was true I could have turned myself in to a police outpost closer to home, there was no one there to help or protect me. Lars would find a lawyer if I had asked him. The information I had must eventually go to the Pinkertons anyway, so it would be faster and more secure if I brought it to them myself. January seemed confident this fellow Wyatt would provide real help, although he never explained why. There was nothing for it but to trust his plan. As mean and nasty as the old cowboy was, he was quick with a plan.

Actually, I felt a bit giddy. For the first time in my life I was stunningly alone. People travelled through this part of the country all the time, but I was not a *coureur de bois* following long-established trade routes, nor the captain of a ship ferrying goods through the Great Lakes, nor a prospector chasing gold or railway worker laying track, nor even a farmer bringing my harvest to market. I had no crew to help me along my way, no merchant anticipating my arrival. I was not a pioneer woman with her entourage of family and farm implements. No one in the universe knew where I was, and not a soul at my destination knew or cared if along the way I wound up as dinner for the wolves I heard howling nightly.

Why did it never occur to me in my entire life that I could get on a horse and go somewhere?

Wrapped in layers of scarves and coats, I was an eccentric species of wildlife moving through these trees. Over the course of a day, I routinely ran across geese and rabbits, less often elk or deer. As we crossed each other's paths, we allowed for a wide berth. I had to rein in Abe to a stop for a bear up ahead that wanted to cross the track. So fierce and wild an animal could have reared up on his hind legs, even charged at me for having the effrontery to come upon him in an unsuspecting moment. Instead, he bent his head down and ambled into the bush with that peculiar bear gait I would describe as hind legs more committed to running than the front ones. Although the animals must have witnessed my encumbrances of clothing, bedroll, and tent, so far my lack of hide and fur served up no reason for interference.

I cogitated about whether these animals even noticed the few railway men who must have shown up one day, dragging survey glasses and maps along with them as they measured and analyzed the landscape. If the animals missed remarking the first wave of these men, they must surely have heard the second wave that returned with axes and dynamite. Crews of railway workers pitched tents along this very section of track to live among the railway ties piled up in awkward hillocks at regular intervals. I could almost hear the howl of Van Horne's saws and the regular beat of the sledgehammers as his men pounded steel into the heart of a continent.

January advised against travelling on a road because its course was unpredictable unless you knew it well. A compass was useless in distinguishing among routes that might all go in the same general direction but led differentially to bogs, lakes, or damaged bridges. He was right that the detour to the Canadian Pacific tracks was worth the extra time and trouble. Train tracks were epic; they overrode details like meandering paths around this inconvenient tree or that obstructive rock. Should an unexpected storm dump too much snow for an individual horse to travel, the plow engine could be depended upon to eventually clank its armour down the track. Should I wander off course, its whistle would call me home.

Even better news about following the tracks, January maintained, was the increased control you had over your own exposure to the rest of the world. On the road, other riders were more likely to happen upon you when you might not want to be happened upon, or may well wait for you in ambush. A train announced itself, first with the whistle and then with coughs and hisses. Anyone seeking cover had plenty of time to arrange it. I had yet to discover anyone else using these tracks as a road.

I was pleasantly surprised that this trip was not nearly so difficult and uncomfortable as I had expected. Perhaps January was a better teacher than I credited him, since I was exhilarated at every turn by my preparedness for the fairly predictable challenges that presented themselves. Next month would bring many feet of snow and piercing arctic winds, the prospects of which no longer frightened me. Nothing could be worse than feeling trapped in that dank shack, haunted by Father's suffering. Out here in my unmitigated freedom, I had to keep pinching myself that this vast expanse was really mine to explore.

January advised that, whenever I wanted to make camp, I should scavenge a few of the evergreen saplings around me, as common here as shells on a seashore. Once I tied them into a rough tent structure, I was to draw over it the tarpaulin he bequeathed to me. Instantly, I had a natural shelter from snow and wind. If the night proved too cold to sleep, I was to build a fire, throw rocks into it until they were hot, then use his thick leather gloves to roll the rocks into my tent. In no time I would have a heated bedroom meriting the envy of anyone climbing into bed in England. Once I doused the fire, I covered the tent with more evergreen branches and disappeared safely under the brush.

I once asked January what he thought about during all those hours of silence and solitude while riding by himself.

—Where to camp. What to eat.

—Surely planning your day does not consume the entire day.

—How not to get killed by whoever's following you.

—Were you always pursued by someone?

—Travelin' always throws something at you to figure out. You think it's going to be peaceful, but it ain't. Don't let yourself get comfortable.

I hoped I was not letting down my guard by reading from the pile of newspapers I brought. As luck would have it, I discovered in my bag a series of articles on the building of this very railway. In a shower of sunshine, Abe clopped along wooden slats against the offbeat staccato of Pinkerton's hooves while I learned that the first section of track for this enormous CPR route was laid across the prairies at an incredible pace of five hundred miles in one season. Sections in Ontario took longer because they required blasting through Laurentian granite. Railway blasters had since gone west to unleash their fury under mountains grumpily dedicated to blocking the train's preferred trail through the Rockies.

I saw that a celebration of the railway's completion was planned for next month. There would be lines of tents with workers cooking over fires as their supervisors' voices called out final instructions. One article suggested the most dangerous work for this railway was done by Chinese dynamite specialists. I remembered a man in Lars's store using the phrase "doesn't have a Chinaman's chance" which I now understand calculated the odds a Chinese dynamiter had of going into a mountain and coming out alive. How driven they must have been to do the hazardous work white men did not dare, all the while receiving less than white men's pay. Getting lost in other peoples' problems distanced me from my own.

New biting winds kicked up, making reading and note-taking impossible. My concentration was lashed to the task of keeping my face wrapped in a kerchief that made me look like I was about to rob a train, an image January likely anticipated on those long nights at the Range staring up at the stars. How much time he spent alone! With my knit hat scrunched down over my eyebrows, and kerchief tied up tightly over my nose, I could see only a sliver of the landscape before me, which did not really matter. Abe knew his marching orders were to stay on the tracks.

I thought about how small my room was back in England. As a child, I adored my narrow bed and overhanging canopy as a worthy abode for a princess. We English were bound to the quaint and cosy. My writing table was no larger than my book or piece of writing paper, and yet it kept me bolted to the floor for hour after hour, unaware of any connection between the tight perimeter of my living space and the extent of the paths I might etch in my mind.

Our parlour often housed friends and relatives all singing together and celebrating occasions without a thought to spilling into the outdoors for the sake of looking at the sky or walking down the middle of the street. Outdoors meant fieldstone walls delineating narrow streets. While a gate might open onto a wider prospect, there would be no hope of new possibility or discovery. For centuries, each farmer shouldered the yoke of the last farmer to till again what had already been long tilled. People like Mother who did not emigrate were likely to travel no more than a few miles beyond where they were born and would die. But here in this behemoth of a country, I could easily travel an entire day and night over land never tilled at all. What must overwhelming space do to the imagination of the people who cope with it?

One pastime I developed on this journey was that of envisioning each tree as a person. I was not alone in the middle of nowhere but rather at the centre of a colossal ball. One morning I crawled out of my brush tent to a world glittering in snow. January would never think of this scene as the result of a cosmic fairy godmother's bag of tiny diamonds given to a daughter charged with decorating the land of Christmas trees below. Some trees were more becoming to dress because they were noticeably taller and more voluminous, grown to full height on a fertile patch of forest floor where they were lucky enough to have a clear shaft up to the sunshine. The less lucky grew smaller, too weak to win elbow room, and so had to make do with whatever they could reach for themselves. Every so often a fully dressed tree stood apart from the crowd with the sunshine on her lace fragmented into a million sparkling droplets.

January would no doubt grunt that I was a ridiculous woman for mucking up reality with idiotic descriptions. Trees were either a refuge from or harbinger of hungry animals and desperate men. I should remain vigilant, ready for a sudden change of plan. And yet, even as constant danger was my reality, I felt only sapped by an unrelenting focus on fears. Survival was surely motivated by what we did with reality.

If January failed to see the north as crowds of beautiful ladies dressed for a ball, what did he make of the colours around him? I noticed three that dominated this country. First there was white, the colour of purity back home, but here the image of frosty sugar over frozen water, or a thick blizzard of flour from a mill in the Milky Way.

I used to think of the colour green as a natural habitat folded into layered shades and variegated leaves best viewed up close in small specimens. The green of the north, however, went on for days until it hardened into a solid wall and left one panting for a disruptive red or shocking purple, even a different shade of green. While the temperatures encouraged extremes, they were not likely to last long. Passions were quickly subdued by arctic temperatures, just as deep freezes were inevitably melted by a compassionate thaw. Finally there was blue, on sunny days the colour spanning 180 degrees of the world, while on other days a mere wink of water through a crowd of branches.

There were also hues of sunlight I once thought invisible but now saw as ranging from yellow mist on a humid sunny day to the steel grey of an angry rain. Father used to read me explorer fantasies about magic polar bears and talking sea creatures. I thought these images outrageous and fantastical. Now they seemed like empty shells trapped in a washed-out imagination in the face of reality's staggeringly vibrant kaleidoscope.

January wanted me to skirt Winnipeg by turning south along the tracks into Minnesota. Soon enough I could catch a train to meet up with the Buffalo Bill show, usually on tour somewhere across the northeastern states. As I got closer to any city, whether I skirted it or otherwise, I might arouse people's curiosity. January was right about how much mental time was taken with plotting one's next move, but I was going to go against his advice for a day or two for the sake of stashing some of his money in a safe place.

What a burden it was to have unwanted money! Now I spent my days plotting what to do with January's packs of bills to keep them safe until I handed everything over to this Shea Wyatt. If I were discovered with this money ahead of time, many would not believe my intention to turn it in. Transferring it out of the saddlebags would cause as much inquisitiveness as carrying the bags around with me. Even if I found a place to stow them temporarily, I would worry about someone becoming suspicious and investigating their contents. I took inspiration from the lion-tamer who thrust his head into the beast's maw. There was nothing to be done but plunge myself straight into a bank, deposit at least some of the money, and arrange for its transfer later.

The money would prove more complicated for anyone to steal if I spread it out over several banks, though I was afraid to put it in an American bank. Stolen American dollars might be traceable in America. I should have asked January. My recurring waking nightmare was a bank clerk peering at me over his glasses to take in a long, hard look before retreating to the back office where he alerted his boss that a woman out front wanted to deposit money stolen by Jesse James.

I planned to blame Father if the money was discovered as stolen, deflect suspicion by calling this money my inheritance. If these were his bills, no one would blame a trusting daughter. Without knowing my father, they would never know the idea was utterly preposterous.

January told me that when the gang decided to plan a robbery, the first thing they did was send four or five men who installed themselves for several days in the vicinity of the bank. They drifted in separately to different hotels and farms that welcomed travellers, raising no flags that a gang was quietly invading. They invented themselves as civil engineers passing through to assess the feasibility of railway routes, or as stockmen dealing in horses and cattle, or simply as land speculators. They asked about existing railway routes, requested maps of roads, expressed interest in landscape details like streams, swamps, and forests, all in keeping with questions expected of potential investors. Even questions about unusual cliffs, swamps, or special landmarks arose as natural points of interest. The welcoming townsfolk could never have foreseen this information constituting the building blocks of a getaway plan. I was not going to rob anyone, but I did have a plan to deposit stolen money in a bank. I needed to fade into the background.

Once settled in my hotel room very near the main intersection of downtown Winnipeg by the river, I soon became conscious of the fact that the entire populace was held spellbound by Riel. In the dress shop the ladies were talking, and at the bar in the hotel restaurant the men were talking, all remembering his first rebellion so close by. The French population, a significant presence here, was terribly upset he was to be hanged. They recounted stories of his channelling the heavens through a crucifix raised high above his head all through the battle at Batoche. Dumont was panegyrised for keeping the thunderous cannon firepower and thousands of Canadian soldiers at bay for three days. Amidst any disapproval about the rebellion, there remained a kind of admiration for the men involved.

This hotel sported a prominent "Ladies Welcome" sign, somewhat repudiated by the odd looks I received when people concluded there was no husband or father with me. I appeared well-to-do with my two horses, which afforded me some protection, but a woman riding alone was clearly not something they saw every day. First I would have the bath I had been craving since Wabigoon, and return myself to a recognizably proper woman. My next order of business was to buy a dress at one of the shops I had spied quickly along the main street. If I were to present myself as a well-situated young heiress, I had best look the part.

By morning, each time I thought about what might happen at

the bank, I began to gasp for breath. To distract myself, I bought a newspaper in the hotel lobby and hurried back to my room much the way I used to do from Lars's store to our shack. Riel was still on the front page, I saw, where correspondents most rabid about hanging him changed their tune when they focused on Dumont, who was safely over the American border. They sang his praises, as though building him up made Middleton more of a hero for winning the day. It must have been a bitter pill for Ottawa to swallow the news that American President Cleveland would not hand Dumont over on the grounds that he was a political prisoner. The fact that Riel was left behind continued to stoke speculation about Dumont returning to effect an eleventh-hour rescue before the noose did its work.

By noon I had my dress, a lavender bustle affair never to be worn again, unless as a costume in Bill Cody's Wild West Show, perhaps as a victimized white woman passenger in their famous Deadwood stagecoach chase routine. When I rustled my skirts into the bank, my major concerns alternated between my knees buckling under me and my balance giving way.

Seeing there was no lineup, I hesitated at the high railing that separated the desks. A teller beckoned me forward. I walked straight to his desk, meditating on why the job of counting money should necessarily imbue a pasty complexion, emaciated body, and nervous tics. I was one to talk. This gaunt young man must certainly have noticed my own jitters as I explained what I wanted: an account that would allow me to forward the balance to another city at some point in the future. When he asked me to repeat my stipulations, I felt the need to explain myself.

—I am a British immigrant. I settled in Wabigoon, about halfway between here and Lakehead.

He rewarded me with a heartening, if ever so slight, lessening of the tautness around his mouth. I interpreted this as a sign of his relief that I was not a complete stranger to the vicinity.

—My father recently died, I offered, encouraged. He did not want me to carry around my inheritance in cash.

—Entirely reasonable sentiment on his part. You have yet to consider your future prospects. You are on your way to meet a husband?

—Goodness, no. I am a teacher. I plan to settle wherever I find a congenial population wishing to be educated.

His head nodded for many seconds at a time, which I mistook as evidence of an argument well made.

I should have shut up while the going was good but, intoxicated with my evident success in gaining his confidence, I recklessly threw in more details than were necessary. When I revealed my plan to head south to the United States, my narrative switched onto a runaway track.

—Will you be taking the St. Paul, Minneapolis, and Manitoba Railway?

—Why no, I will be riding my horse, just as I have done from Wabigoon to here.

That bit of information sentenced me to replay this mistake in my mind for years to come in the hopes of retraining my nature to be more circumspect and cautious, even when—especially when— things are going well. Had I not spoken from impulse, I might have reasoned that such a pinched-looking face belied deeply entrenched arrogance about anyone other than himself competently devising and executing a plan. He bundled up my money quickly once I had signed the signature card.

—This rough country is no place for a woman riding a horse alone.

I should have anticipated the reaction, except that having already spent so many days as a woman travelling alone in rough country, I had become sloppy about remembering what was impossible for a woman. I now appreciated this must be what January meant by getting comfortable. Come to think of it, though, he did not give much thought to how this whole travelling and surviving business would be different for me in towns. January had likely never experienced bank personnel worrying about his travel plans.

—There are men with evil intentions in cities as well, the clerk conceded, but you would not be able to hold your own if confronted in the wilderness. There is a perfectly serviceable rail line south from Winnipeg and onto Minneapolis.

—I am aware of that particular utility, Sir, but I prefer to ride my horse. I have two horses, and find it easiest to travel with them to my destination. I prefer an outdoor life.

Even though this sounded perfectly rational to my own ears, he regarded me with the incredulity of someone gawking at a ghost yet still unable to believe it. Why did I not think to just nod and agree with him? Horrified, I watched the scene I had envisioned as my worst nightmare unfold before my eyes. A suspicious teller retreated to an office at the back of the bank to consult with someone. The boss came out, more suspenders and spectacles, his back rigid straight. He spoke as though to a child or someone who did not speak English.

—You must understand our concern for your safety, Miss. We cannot in good conscience send an innocent out into danger. A woman travelling unescorted is in a precarious position no matter what the mode of travel, but the worst would be alone and on horseback. Allow us to check for train schedules.

My assurance that they need not be concerned sparked intransigence in them, which then ignited resentment in me. Despite my haughtiest exhortations, nothing restrained their objections. It dawned on me that all the while I was insisting that I knew what I was doing on a horse in the bush, my bustle and dainty gloves told them otherwise. January could have deployed me usefully in his bank robberies, in that he could have hauled out the entire safe from the vault while I merely asked if I could open an account and get back on my horse.

Throughout the time the teller and his boss competed as surrogate fathers falling over each other to make alternate arrangements for me and my horses on a train, I could see the strands of a web winding around this distraught daughter, too fragile to make sensible plans now that she had no supervision. This kind of woman needed a Lars. I wished I could pull out the Pinkerton's overgrown rifle and shoot out each of the lights above us as though they were pigeons, just to shock these two fussy men back onto their stools. I forced myself to focus on January's admonition: above all else, avoid attracting attention. Too late, I shifted gears to smile and nod as though perfectly open to a change in plan.

The silver lining in all this was that they quickly processed and ferried my money into the depository with not so much as a second thought. But, in short order, my business was bandied around the bank until it reached a gaggle of Mennonite immigrants, all dressed in black, come to do their banking in town. Two of the taller men with black beards, hats, and suits approached me and said in thick Russian accents that they could not accept anything but my accompanying them south to their village to teach English to their people!

One of the men, who addressed me as "younk voman" and was apparently accustomed to making decisions for those around him, dispatched several of the quiet and patient-looking women—black bonnets, black dresses to their ankles, hands gnarled from work in the fields—to surround me in a show of hospitality. Once they discovered I could be useful to them and protected by them at the same time, all was arranged. I would accompany them with my horses south from Winnipeg in the direction of the US. Instead of continuing on my way alone, however, I would stay with them and teach them how to conduct their business more accurately with the English-speaking community surrounding them. They had much to learn, or so their bows graciously insisted, and I had much to teach.

Sitting on Abe, I waited in resignation for the endless packing-up process. After the bank, they shopped through the feed and general stores, the women talking quietly to the men, and the men going into the stores to do the business. Everyone watched as the sacks and baskets of supplies were loaded into their carts. I waited, silently rehearsing to myself that this sacrifice was the one step back that would eventually allow two steps forward. As long as I had the horses and my guns, they could not keep me prisoner.

From that perspective, I was getting out of Winnipeg quietly, headed in the right direction on horseback with ten thousand dollars safely deposited in the bank. I would follow January's advice to be inventive and adaptable when faced with unexpected obstacles. He said a delay was not a problem if it handed me a ticket to ride out clear, although I suspect delay to him was more likely an extra whiskey and a poker game.

By early afternoon, after packing up my belongings and still wearing my prim dress, I sat decorously sidesaddle atop my remaining twenty thousand American dollars. I rode captive across the prairie alongside a mournful wagon train of silent Mennonites, hypothesizing about whether Abe knew or cared that we had just been commandeered. This cowgirl was not in control as January would have been. I considered spurring Abe into a gallop to leave my well-meaning chaperones in my dust. In a few short minutes, I could be out in the open and speeding toward the border. I half expected to see Lars ride up behind us, his Swedes and Finns in tow, intent on dragging me back. I hated being patient, hated it. Be that as it may, if I acted impetuously now, I would be too easily classified as a runaway woman horse rider with something to escape. Unwanted community is a woman's plague.

Over the next weeks and months, I learned more than I ever wanted to know about Russian Mennonite farmers. Enticed here by Canadian officials with the promise of hundreds of acres of land, these farmers of the steppes fulfilled their promise to settle along the border to form a natural blockade against Americans bent on running roughshod over all limitation. From what I gathered, Mennonite lives were unglamorous in every aspect. During the spring, summer, and fall, they broke and cultivated land, brought in what food they could, and prepared for winter. In these winter months they made and repaired clothing, bedding, furniture, farm implements—and for a dose of excitement, learned English. They cared for the animals and processed whatever food they produced—drying, canning, and so on. In this constant toil, I saw no evidence of merrymaking, no musical instruments, artwork, or even embroidery.

Evidently, these people could survive anywhere. I would lay money on their village back in Russia looking and functioning exactly as the one they created here. I had to admit, though, the huts were better than our shack in Wabigoon. Although spare and basic, there was a rough charm to the mud and stick walls that made one feel enveloped in an earthen womb.

From outside, pale lilac mud walls fringed by a thatched roof created the impression that this was an abode of elves. Particularly charming were the window sashes washed in a muted red pigment, anchoring a set of functional shutters that—perhaps unwittingly— sneaked in a soft grey. The huts must have looked stunning in the early fall when pale fields of crops reflected a yellow haze of soft sunshine. Honestly, this description was more what I wanted it to be than what was, since no one who saw these huts up close would mistake them for anything but basic rural hovels.

Just as the land back in Wabigoon was rockier than Father and I had expected, this prairie land was not what the Mennonites had expected, although they seemed far less precious about their disappointment. In fact they expressed no disappointment at all. While I wanted nothing to do with my fields of rock, these people applied their farming knowledge to the daunting task of draining a prairie swamp, a horrendously backbreaking effort, to produce arable land. Their experience here was brand new as individual farmers and as immigrants, for they were several generations removed from those who actually broke the land back home. Canada promised they would not be bothered for their religious beliefs, which from what I saw was a promise kept, prompting me to question whether Canada could pass a law to make people mind their own business when a single woman put money in the bank and wished to ride her horse alone through the wilderness.

I noticed that the women had little to say for themselves when the men were in the room, not that it affected me as the outsider teacher. The men saw me as the equivalent of a farm implement, while the women took their more surreptitious opportunities to stroke the silk material of my dress. There was nothing more desolate than living outside a culture that surrounded you. I almost wished a religion upon myself, if only to connect to all the praying that went on around me. Praying and working and praying and working, a little eating and learning English, and then back to praying and working.

Living among people unable to speak English did come with its benefits. Obviously inquisitive about me, they struggled to find English words for questions about my background and plans. I admitted to understanding only the questions I wished to answer, or those that did not involve revealing too much. Our interactions were mostly about naming things: I pointed to a chair and said the word, and they told me the Russian word. These were a practical people who apprehended that, no matter how much they would like to hold the heathen world around them at bay, they needed to do business with it. I asked the men to bring newspapers from town whenever they went, promising to teach them how to read the financial and farm news.

I found myself picturing what Lars must have done the day I was late to come and teach the Swedes on the Monday afternoon after I left. Less likely to just walk in now that I was grieving and alone, he would have knocked on the door of our shack, perhaps come back later a couple of times, thinking I had trekked off to practise my shooting, until he became concerned that I might be in distress. I speculated on how long he waited before he opened the door to find my note. His dreams must have crashed around him as he walked back to students who no doubt waited for him expectantly at their rough desks. How quiet it all must have been when he related the news that their school no longer had a teacher. My stomach sickened thinking of their confused faces, not to mention his sense of betrayal that I was not going to help him build his dream.

I held court in my own mind. I would have divulged my plans had I felt safe from anyone trying to stop me or, worse, bringing in the police. My mind ran forward to stew about whether or not they discovered my secret. So long as they never thought to start poking around the Range with shovels—and why would they even think of it, really?—my secret should last as long as I allowed it to last. It was my conscience that had difficulty bearing the weight of it over time.

Worry followed me here from Wabigoon. What if one of my relatives from back home sent a letter? Lars would then have an address. He was just the kind of well-meaning citizen to write back on the presumption I had returned to England. He would express his condolences about Father to people who did not yet know he was gone. They might well jump to the conclusion I ran off into the wilderness to do away with myself out of grief. Maybe they would contact the North-West Police to come looking for me. I tried to head all this off in my note to him by making it known I had gone to a city in the United States, where I had old friends. Lars might have believed this, but my relatives would spot the lie.

When I first came here to live with the Mennonites, I told them of my desire to practise shooting, which in turn caused considerable alarm. They could not understand why I wanted to shoot a gun. As the days and weeks dragged on, with my rifle wrapped up and stowed under my bed, I thought about it less frequently, like a loved one's face sinking into time. It has been so long now, whatever skill I developed under January's tutelage must be badly atrophied. I ached to practise my shooting. A while ago I toyed with the idea of going back to

Wabigoon just to be able to shoot again. People would attribute my rash departure to grief unhinging me. My only happiness since coming to this continent, or maybe ever in my life, was what I experienced at the Range with my gun.

A snowfall deep beyond anything I ever experienced pitched me into new despair. For weeks I moved through my days like an automaton until, without warning, mournfulness engulfed me. Memories of Father lurked dormant until regret sprang to life full blown to perpetrate its assault on my equilibrium. I was flooded with memories prompted by images of parents and children in natural domestic circumstances, where a mother might hand something out of reach to her small child or sing the snippet of a song that soothed discomfort. Sometimes I perceived the shape of Father's hands in my own as I cradled a tea mug. I thought of his breathless voice, his tormented eyes.

I took out his pocket compass and stared at the inscription again: *So that you can always find your way back to me.* I envied those who opened their Bible or favourite book to a random passage they believed capable of channelling prophetic guidance. I opened the compass, anticipating that *north* might leap out at me, meaning I should head back to Father and Wabigoon. If I were to go north, I might one day congratulate myself on having had the foresight to work hard for solid, salt-of-the-earth people. Either that, or I might regret having settled for Lars and the kind of life I would have to have there.

I sat with the Mennonite women after dinner, four or five of us at the cleared rough-plank table. They darned and mended as I huddled up to the lantern to read old newspapers, much like I did in Wabigoon. I thought of reading aloud to them, but listening to English was hard, and this was their time of day to sit and work peacefully. Where did their minds go when free to wander? Did farmers dream of jumping on a horse and racing away somewhere new, or were their imaginations chained to the gruel that must be made in the morning? Everything I read took me somewhere else. And yet, much as my mind wanted to go, my body remained listless.

Into our silent room walked a little boy I knew to be around ten years old. I had taught him a few words when he showed interest, although he was noticeably shy around me. He approached with something in each hand. The first hand offered up my journal. My shock frightened him. I had stowed the journal in an outside pocket of the saddlebag under my bed. He must have been exploring. Had he pursued his curiosity much further, he might be offering up fistfuls of the twenty thousand dollars stuffed under my bed beside my rifle. If I made too big a fuss about his bringing me things from my room, the adults might grow suspicious about what I had to hide. I hurried to reply "thank you," which I had taught him, so he would know I was not angry.

The mothers looked up, sniffing for trouble. I smiled and made encouraging noises to the boy, more to reassure the women. The boy stepped back, sought out his mother's lap and began to whimper. I smiled at the mother, held up my journal, and repeated "thank you," which prompted her to admonish the boy gently to come forward and make friends. He slid off her lap and returned to me tentatively. He thought he was giving me something important, which he was. This was a record of my life before becoming bogged down here with his family members. He must have believed my good will because he then offered what was in his other hand, a newspaper. The men had gone to town, and his father likely sent him as delivery boy. I clapped my hands to show I was pleased. The women smiled and nodded to each other, and then to him. I motioned for him to come and sit beside me at the table, where I smoothed out a blank page in my journal. Fishing out a pencil from my pocket, I wrote "newspaper" to show what he had given me. We repeated it to each other several times before I strung together the sentence "thank you for the newspaper." Although the smile of recognition that broke over his face made me want to hug him, I restrained myself in case it was inappropriately demonstrative. Instead, I made a show of reading the newspaper to convince him how much I appreciated having it.

Articles about Louis Riel's hanging still dominated the front pages. I honed in on an article about Gabriel Dumont's brother, interviewed in his sanctuary in the United States. He said they knew very well Riel was insane. Before Riel turned himself in to General Middleton, the Dumonts and others had been searching for days with the intention of tying their leader to a horse and whisking him off, whether he wanted to go or not. Some said Riel actively evaded Dumont so as not to be found. In handing himself over to Middleton, he guaranteed himself either the public platform for his day in court or the ecstasy of martyrdom.

At first I succeeded in silently and discreetly wiping away my tears, until sobs surged up my throat to announce my despair to the Mennonite world, wracking me into a shudder no matter how hard I tried to suppress the sounds. Women jumped to their feet, thinking I had read something upsetting in the paper. Even if language were not a barrier between us, I would have had difficulty explaining that it was not Louis Riel's death that unravelled me. It was the running aground of his dream.

If he had stopped too soon, he would never have achieved the success of the first rebellion. If he had not gone on so long, he would have avoided the failure of the second. How can you tell if your dreams will shipwreck you before they ever reach open water? Successes come from great risks; failures come from harebrained gambles. How is one to know the difference between heroic perseverance and foolish clinging?

As the women patted my shoulder, I berated myself for running off with stolen money and lethal guns to do an unnecessary job of returning what was not mine and testifying to events I could have let slide into nothingness. One dead man in the newspaper translated in my mind to the three I left buried in Wabigoon. Here I was, bereft again, in worse condition and more alone than ever in my life.

With a shawl around my shoulders and a warm mug in my hands, I thanked sympathetic faces before leaving the hut for my own room. I smiled and said thank you again to the boy, who was now so thoroughly confused he would probably never again deliver my paper. I recognized in their faces the same look I saw in the bankers' faces, who probably told the Mennonites about Father. They likely assumed I was still lonely and grieving, and they were not wrong. They just did not know how much there was to grieve.

The Mennonites gave me two stalls in the barn for Abe and Pinkerton. Whatever desperate pleasure I eked out of a day came from mucking out these stalls and exercising each horse. I took Pinkerton first, for no other reason than he inhabited the stall closest to the door. Once I finished cleaning, riding, and feeding him, I moved on to Abe, the horse I felt really belonged to me. Lately Abe was in a huff as I led him out of his stall. He had taken to nipping me on the shoulder. Perhaps he was jealous, or anxious to go. No wonder January wanted to holler at him. For a horse, he had some fairly definite judgments, whether I understood them accurately or not.

Careful to ride sidesaddle until I got out of sight, I then changed to straddle position and opened him up into a full gallop. The experience of riding was all that enlivened me to go on. Abe charged along windswept paths between ploughed fields booby-trapped with deeper snow. Farmland was an effective jailer. It connected ploughed lots together like cells. Only corridors of space between them could be depended on for hard terrain.

The day I opened the newspaper and saw Buffalo Bill Wild West Show leap off the page, I was jolted all the more because I had for so long forgotten about looking for it. My hand trembled as though disembodied from me while I ran my finger down the schedule: Missouri, Indiana, Ohio, West Virginia, Maryland, Washington,

Philadelphia, and finally New York in late June, when they would set up for a six-month stint, three months on Staten Island and three in Madison Square Gardens. From my study of the Pinkerton's maps, New York looked too ambitious a distance to attempt by horse, but I could be anonymous in New York.

On the way back to my hut after another silent dinner with the Mennonites, I quite suddenly looked up. Not a shred of cloud obscured my view of the constellations hanging over me. There was the North Star at the end of the Little Dipper's handle, exactly where it was supposed to be, there for eons in the same place despite fathers dying, cowboys showing up out of nowhere, and nothing feeling familiar or comforting anymore or ever again. The night was alarmingly bright with light that may have emanated from the stars sprayed from one horizon to the other, or maybe from the mirror effect of moonlight bouncing back off the snow. Either way, it illuminated the fact that there was no shackle clasped to my ankle, no bar preventing my exit.

I left the Mennonites a note. Not an exceptionally informative one, but one giving them the impression that I had relatives to meet who would take care of me, and entreating them not to worry. They would be less likely to send out a rescue party if they felt another community had stepped up to take responsibility for me. I used only the words I had taught them to make sure they would understand what I was communicating. I dragged my saddles and saddlebags out to the stable where Abe snorted, exasperated I had taken this long. I tethered Pinkerton's reins to Abe's saddle so that we could all ride in a line. Mounted and in full gallop toward the railway tracks, I debated still which direction I would choose.

We raced shadows out to the limits of our vision, where striated shades of a grey-toned rainbow sank into the black distance. Once I recognized the familiar lines of steel etched into the snow-like lines of ink on a blank page, I turned south toward the United States of America. Apparently I was incorrigible. Bruised and terrified, lonely and misspent, here I was again on the road to what frightened me most.

SIX

ARRIVED

I struck camp in a sheltered area of northern Minnesota, up on a ridge that surveyed miles of landscape with no evidence of human habitation. After a week, I was still practising what I learned from January, galloping at full speed on Abe while Pinkerton watched us with apparent contentment from his post tied to a tree. Abe was either as energized as I was to be on the move again, or he was showing off to Pinkerton. I marked my perimeter with targets of treetops as I streaked around my gigantic natural track. After months of flapping about in my own mind, I now let loose my own personal goblins and guardian angels to pursue me at breakneck speed around and around in the open wilderness.

Huddled over my campfire, my overwrought energy spent on riding and shooting until every part of me ached, I conceded I was nowhere near good enough to secure employment in a wild-west show. The biggest advantage January gave me, oddly enough, was the recognition of my own limitations. Those people in Cody's show likely learned to wield guns and ride horses before they learned to walk. I would need much more practise on a horse to make up for a lifelong deficit.

When I fell asleep that night, I dreamt I was dressed up in my bustled lavender dress, not at the front door of the Winnipeg bank, but at the entrance to the Stillwater Prison, four hundred or so miles south where I knew the Younger brothers were still incarcerated. As is often the case in dreams, there was no explanation of why I was there. I told the warden's men at the gate that I wished to speak to Cole Younger, giving the excuse that I was with the organization lobbying to pardon him.

Although the guard opened the gate, he apparently felt compelled to comment that murderers were best left in jail, to which I responded that I supposed the people qualified to make that decision would determine who was a murderer. He pointed in the direction I needed to go to the visiting room, where I sat convinced they were preparing a cell for me. A man emerged, his flinty eyes reminding me of January as he slumped into the chair across the table.

I told him I had a message for him from January, intimating that the gun had to remain in my purse so as not to risk the guards' notice. His silence gave me no clue about whether he was proud of his fellow gang member or jealous that January was never caught. Before I knew it, he had the gun in his hand, my arm bent behind my back, and the barrel pointed at my temple. In a few desperate moments he dragged me down the stairs with guards' guns trained on both of us. In the moment I was sure I was about to die in a shootout, I risked all and broke for freedom. Somehow I magically reached Abe, who knew to race back around the way no one would expect, Pinkerton right behind us unbidden yet running for his life. I held onto the saddle without attempting to steer. Abe was the one who would decide where we should go. That was the bulk of the dream, me racing through unknown terrain, terrified by what must be behind me, clinging to a mute animal for my destiny.

I awoke from this dream to three Indians staring down at me. In my zeal to find a place to practise shooting and riding, I had apparently chosen campsites far enough away from the railroad track to land me on a reservation. Respectful but insistent, they escorted me to the tracks. I pointed on one of my maps where I had been and where I wanted to go. They understood the map perfectly well, and assured me I was going in the right direction. I was relieved they did not try to put me on a train.

My chivalrous bank teller back in Winnipeg would have been pleased to learn that I finally did buy a ticket of my own accord for his St. Paul, Minneapolis and Manitoba Railway. Drowsing to the relentless clack of the wheels, I was periodically startled awake by the whistle's announcement of our arrivals as we approached the various stations spread along this relatively new track. That sound I once regarded as desolate now made me think of Abe and Pinkerton, safely stowed a few boxcars behind me, all three of us now speeding through American countryside to our future. I could tell our exact direction because I had my compass sitting open on the little train table in front of me. I followed its every permutation as we curled toward the south or turned back east as we went. From this window, I would never have guessed that I had passed into another country, the third one now this compass had seen.

Newspapers were suddenly crammed with advertisements for the Bill Cody Wild West Show. In the illustration, Cody's face smiled from beneath his signature wide white hat. His goatee completed an image that had become iconic to most in these parts. I found myself dwelling on where he got the idea for so extravagant a production and why his fellow Americans exulted in these stories. Despite controlling most of the globe, Britain never thought to stage such theatrics about its expansion.

Alongside these advertisements, there were articles crediting Bill Cody with being a good friend to the Indians, proved by their willingness to work for him. I found this a bit peculiar, since the plot of his show was always the same. The Indians raced after the Deadwood stagecoach, whooping and firing their guns, only to have the cowboys save the day by overtaking them. This story of loss was a dispiriting one to act out day after day. Cody was rumoured to be thinking of staging Custer's last stand, perhaps as an expression of respect for Sitting Bull and his surviving Sioux.

If circumstances demanded, I might find lodging for the horses to facilitate my attendance at the show each day, even though that would necessitate dipping into the money I intended to give back. January did make the point that I was entitled to cover my expenses for the trip. Or, I could give journalism a whirl and write an article about the show as I experienced it. That would justify nosy questions to various troupe members after the show. Better, though, would be the odd innocent question posed by a trusted fellow co-worker.

After the bizarre dream I had in Minnesota, it heartened me to hear that the Younger brothers languished yet behind bars in Stillwater, despite efforts on their behalf to have them paroled or pardoned. One of their champions claimed a Younger brother saved his life during the Civil War. An outlaw was a breaker of rules, while a hero fought for right regardless of the rules, and these two actions apparently shaved rather close to each other on occasion, like Robin Hood.

As I sat watching miles of trees stream by, I became preoccupied with this train that hurtled me across a new land. In England, the building of a railway pitched those who wanted to get their products to market against those who feared the poor would flood London or, worse, eddy out to smaller towns where the children of the rich were installed in boarding schools. With hindsight of trains having existed for decades, it was apparent that they actually helped everyone. Coal and farm products got to the coast faster, fish got to the interior, the rich started holidaying in seaside places, and the poor could travel more easily. I did not recall complaints of school children becoming more endangered.

In North America, the railway was a different beast. Transcontinental. Nation-building. For Macdonald, the train bound three seas together as a bulwark against the Americans. For the Americans, it was a way to reattach itself as a nation ripped apart by civil war. For Riel's Métis and the Indians, it was a harbinger of Macdonald's Canada and the disappearance of the buffalo. For Shep January and his James Gang, it represented another force of northern domination over the south, but at least it did so as a travelling bank. January said the only money they really wanted from a train was the contents of its safe. Anything they did with the passengers was merely sport, distraction while the safe was blown.

In the early days, the gang members made a show of identifying passengers who hailed from the south. Grandstanding gentlemanly honour ensued as the gang asked after their health and assured them no harm would come to their person or property. The northerners, on the other hand, were toyed with for entertainment, often stripped to their underwear while ridiculed and robbed of whatever they carried.

Rolling open spaces slowed to New York City's multi-storied buildings, high and proud, pressed up against wide main streets. These were not main streets scratched out of wagon wheel paths, nor medieval routes twisting around a big city like London, but straight vistas racing boldly north into the distance. Overhead, telephone, telegraph, and power lines crisscrossed, as though some cosmic loom had woven a buzzing, high-powered ceiling. Everywhere crowds squeezed between ubiquitous vendors. Sizzling fish and sausages wafted from the markets of the lower harbour. Everyone hurried here, whether it was to haul something, or sell something, or meet someone. In a glimpse down an alleyway, I could see children playing barefoot beneath horizontal flagpoles of hanging laundry. The city roiled, impatient, rushing toward the future.

I unloaded my horses from the train and then reloaded them onto the ferry bound for Staten Island. Once on the island, I boarded a small train specially constructed to take livestock, performers, and spectators to the new outdoor arena built for Cody's show. A short ride ushered us into a frenetic environment where hammers rang out from all around, not like in Wabigoon where you could follow the progress of one building at a time. Here buildings rose all around you at once: platoons of men on huge bleacher benches, makeshift barns, fences delineating the inside and outside of the arena. Predictably, people clamoured to pay their money. Who would not want a ticket to share in this gargantuan dream that transformed reality before your eyes?

Once the small train coasted to a stop inside the show's compound, I followed a line of Indians to the stables, where Abe, Pinkerton, and I gawked at the pandemonium. I expected horses but not elk and bison, donkeys and deer. Even a bear! All were unlikely roommates together in this show because they shared the distinction of being animals of the New World. There must have been dozens of employees. Pinkerton reared up at the thundering of an incoming stagecoach pushed by six men. Abe remained unruffled. I looked at him askance, thinking he might be showing off to Pinkerton, but he ignored my scowl.

January would blend into this crowd, camouflaged, slouching languidly on his horse as he waited for the next paroxysm of activity to pass. Everyone wore cowboy hats. Most would welcome an ex-Jesse James Gang gunslinger walking among them. Dangerous characters boosted the allure of the show. Even his southern drawl would have been welcomed as a contribution to the mystique of sworn enemies mingling in a caravan of misfits. He told me to act like I belonged, that people were not nearly so interested in who I was as I might think—unless I gave them reason to get interested.

A skinny man with big cowboy boots and missing teeth stood beside the barn directing traffic.

—Where do you go to get hired on? I called out.

I squelched my instinctive propensity to add "sir" to my salutation, or pepper my phrasing with "please" and "thank you." If my accent did not give me away as an imposter, I feared my pallor and uncalloused hands would. His eyes slid down to my work boots and raised back up to the two horses standing behind me.

—Salsbury, he answered, as though I would know who he meant.

For a moment I stood there, no more enlightened about where I should turn than before our brief interchange. When he inclined his head to indicate that I should follow him, I could almost hear January admonishing me for being in too much of a hurry, opining that people in a rush were usually trying to sell you something. I followed with my horses through double doors into the barn and on to a makeshift office. A small man stooped over a desk.

—Two horses, said the skinny man.

The small man looked up, stirred from his preoccupation. He seemed out of place, as though he had wandered away from his stool in a bank or accountant's office and somehow woke up here. I would have walked by him without notice had he been the one standing outside the barn when I entered the yard.

—Do we need them? he asked.

—Got more cowboys and Indians than horses right now.

Small eyes looked over my shoulder to Abe with Pinkerton. The man looked at me for the first time.

—You want to muck out stalls, we can use your horses.

I could have asked what the pay was, or what days I would work, even where I would sleep and where I would stow my belongings.

—Deal, I said.

Even January would not have expected it to be this swift and uncomplicated. He thought I was going to have to connive from a distance how to worm my way in, maybe even have to try out as a shooter.

I conducted my horses after the skinny man until he pulled open the gate of a stall. Abe snorted his insistence for food and water.

—Put 'em in here. You muck out this stall and the five on the other side. Jake!

In a moment a boy with a mop of black curls hanging over his eyes emerged from a stall across the aisle.

—Give her a fork to feed the horses and show her the tent.

Jake pulled a pitchfork down from the wall, smiling as though shy. He could not be surprised about my being a woman, since I had seen in the throng outside there were many of us about.

—Here's where you can find fresh hay for your horses. Water's over here.

He led me to big barrels and a pile of smaller pails.

—Thank you, Jake.

The barn was comfortingly dim and imbued with muted horse noises as I pitched hay into one trough and filled another with water. By the time Jake took me to a tent set up like a barracks with cots, he seemed comfortable with me. He reminded me of a cat. The less attention paid to him, the more easygoing he became.

It seemed I had employment, board for my horses, and a place to stay in the show. It took all of an hour to make these arrangements. For the price of a horse and a train ticket—which I could have afforded from what Father and I brought with us—this world was available to me at any time I chose.

The fact that I had not spent any of January's money did not relieve me of the ongoing need for a safe place to store it. Saddlebags and guns that were encumbrances on the train were even more of a burden here. I could not very well leave them unattended in the open bunk-room I now shared with transient strangers. I planned to sleep on my saddlebags with guns strategically placed under my pillow and blanket until I could get rid of all this tomorrow.

First thing in the morning, I fed Abe and Pinkerton and mucked out their stalls before leaving for the shuttle train and ferry back to New York. I soon discovered that banks clustered around the harbour, which made sense now that I thought about it. As I walked the streets deciding which bank to choose, I started thinking that it might seem dubious for a stable-hand just hired by Cody to be in need of a bank already. Anxious to avoid the debacle of Winnipeg, I considered more carefully what my story should be this time. I could admit to being a visitor in the United States and explain my money on the basis of wanting to purchase property in New York. There was no need to tell them where I got it. I could claim I had a husband so they would have to deal with me as a woman on her own. But, thinking about it further, I might run into rules about a husband needing to give permission for anything official. To be safe, stories of fathers, husbands, and brothers should be bypassed.

A new costume was in order. Instead of exploring the ladies' dress shops with front windows sporting feathered hats or bunches of silk flowers, I pushed open a door to breathe deeply the combination of gunpowder and leather. In no time I had the same kind of jacket I had noticed several times around the barn at the Cody show, with fringes down the arms and across the shoulders at the back. I threw in two more pairs of men's trousers, work shirts, socks, and another pair of boots. I would leave undergarments for another day.

My boots thumped loudly on the bank's wood floor with the extra weight of my saddlebag slung over my shoulder. A teller glanced up and motioned me toward a wicket. He looked like he might be a cousin of the one in Winnipeg, but in my trousers and leather-fringed jacket, I looked like no relation to that delicate daughter in the dress.

—I would like to rent a safe deposit box, I stated.

—Large or small?

—Large.

He reached for a pamphlet.

—These are the regulations. You'll need to pay the rental for the first three months in advance.

—I will pay for the first year.

Eye contact for the first time.

—You'll be given a key that opens the box in conjunction with a key we keep here at the bank. Fill out the signature card, also indicating anyone else you give permission to open the box.

Who else indeed. My relatives were all across an ocean. I wrote down the name "Shea Wyatt" and handed the card back to the teller.

He conducted me to an anteroom, empty but for a table, where he told me to wait. In a few moments he returned to slide a large strongbox onto the table.

—I will leave you alone for a few minutes. When you have deposited your material in the box, close it, and wave outside the door for me to come back with the keys.

The second he closed the door behind him, I set my saddlebag on the table and took Pinkerton's guns out to pack in one end of the box. Then, I carefully placed January's two Smith & Wesson Schofield .45s at the other end. I buried them both in packets of January's money until I had to lean all my weight on the lid to clamp it down. When I called back the teller and he handed me my key, we clicked the box closed.

—Here is your second key for the other name. Make sure you remember the number of your box.

I nodded and left.

I estimated just under half of my stash fit in the first box. I wanted to use another bank nearby so as not to put all my eggs in one basket. If I were frugal I was sure I could live on the wages I earned from

Cody, whatever they were. The show provided room and board. Come to think of it, apart from a house or piece of property, I really did not know what I would want to buy. In a tent, no matter how big, there was no space for fancy clothes or furniture.

Next day, I set out on the ferry for Manhattan once more and found a new bank around the corner from the one I attended the day before. Without the guns, the remaining ten thousand or so dollars fit with room to spare. When I returned to the stable near noon, Jake threw me a shovel. Chores needed to be finished early for the show's grand opening-day parade the next day. Since the show was located on Staten Island but the parade would take place in Manhattan, everything was scheduled for ferrying to Manhattan first thing in the morning. By early afternoon we would be poised to flood the city with horses, animals, and performers, creating such noise and excitement that throngs of spectators would be sufficiently piqued about what we were up to over here to stream out to Staten Island and visit us.

While I was madly shovelling out my five stalls, Jake called out to me.

—Something is wrong with Annie Oakley! You need to brush down her horse.

I walked out of the stall to find him.

—What is wrong with her?

—I don't know, but everyone is buzzing about her being sick. No one can remember her ever being sick before.

—Jake, everyone has been sick at one time or another.

—Well, she must be in some kinda terrible shape. She always visits her horse before a show, rain or shine. She's famous for never missing a performance.

—Is she going to miss the parade?

—If I know Miss Oakley, she'll make it somehow.

I smiled to myself as I returned to my stall, postulating how well he could know Miss Oakley. If she needed help with the horse, I was more than happy to oblige. He showed me where her horse was, a thorough professional that did not seem to mind who brushed him down.

Once I finished the grooming, Jake came by again to crow about having been right in his prediction.

—Saddle up the horse in the morning because Annie is coming to the parade!

—Where is the blanket to set under her saddle?

—She has a favourite one. You'll need to go to her tent for the one she always uses.

The tent was easy enough to find. Not only was it close by, but there were all sorts of people milling about outside it, talking about a bug that had worked its way into her ear as she slept and weakened her to an alarming degree. The doctors had as yet been unable to dissuade her from riding in the parade. The man at the tent's entrance relayed my request for her blanket to someone inside, who handed it to the man at the door, who handed it out to me. I hurried back to the stables, breathless with excitement. Even though I had yet to see her, I knew where she was and was about to meet her.

This morning, the doctor's prescription to keep Annie in bed demonstrated why she was known as having the will and tenacity of a lion, consistent with her reputation for ignoring rain, hail, sleet, snow, and sniffles. True to Jake's prediction, she followed through on her insistence to have her horse saddled and waiting for her. Jake told me Annie would rather die than let Lillian Smith replace her as the woman shooter in the parade. Much younger and apparently just itching to knock Annie off her perch as best shooter in the show, Lillian came from the frontier in Coleville, California, and liked to call herself the "Champion Rifle Shot of the World." I was frankly astounded there were so many professional women shooters in existence. Annie was in a different category because she was married and lived in a tent with her husband. The others were less distinctive as women largely because they, like me, wore the same attire as the men.

I did not know what I expected Annie Oakley to look like. Myths and legends lived in the rarefied time of long ago, and in the magical realm of far away. It could not be anything but a shock to encounter a legend as a mere two-legged creature looking for her horse. Even though I had heard her described as petite, in my mind she was a tall mountain of a woman who could take up space in a man's world. And so I was taken aback to see that I towered over a figure the size of a child, barely five feet, and slender. Her ashen face struck me as one likely to look thoughtful in health. Her eyes, now glazed with fever, looked quick and intelligent. So fierce was her determination to get on that horse that she noticed no one around her. Frank had evidently resigned himself to helping her up. Not a word was said by any of us.

Once in the saddle with the reins in her hands, Jake and I galloped off with her, flanking each side to keep a protective watch and ensure she met her connection with the train and then the ferry. Once in New York, we kept close behind her with the help of other parade members who acknowledged us as her caretakers by opening up an area around her. By the way she waved and played to the crowds gathered along Broadway to cheer the Cody troupe, I would never have known she was suffering.

Bill Cody rode up front, a spritely man for so big a frame, the epitome of a charming gentleman in his fine white suit. According to Jake, Bill Cody and Annie were not close friends, but they were most cordial. With her calling him "Colonel" and him calling her "Missie," they set a pleasantly professional tone for their fellow performers. The Indians camped together without mingling too much with the other troupe members. The Indian women lived in the Indian section of the show's living areas, while the white women shooters camped together in their own section. Even with these internal divisions, everyone said Cody's show considered itself a family because everyone was pledged to him.

Annie and Cody were the two performers accepted in all camps simply as themselves. Everyone laughed when Cody arrived, partly because his drinking and philandering were legendary, yet the laughter was more affectionate than derisive. Remarkably dedicated to keeping the show on track and successful, he managed to pull himself together for the important situations. He had fought the government to be able to hire as many Indians as he needed, and altered their pay to justify getting them on the show. He did this for Sitting Bull last year.

I shared oogly-eyed wonder with the children in the crowd even though I was the one, incredibly, sitting on Abe at the centre of the parade. January would never have sought out a parade, of this I am sure, which told me Abe was a poker-player of a horse capable of biding his time when trapped. He maintained admirable control, keeping us in line even with his rider distracted by the awestruck crowd that waved, laughed, and called out incomprehensible messages to the cowboys, Indians, stagehands, and general muckers like me. In my most outrageous dreams I could never have conjured up this many different kinds of people moving together in a frontier fairy tale that was also an historical event in its own right.

As I let the scene work its way into my pores, I was arrested by the stare of a man on a horse two parade columns over from me. Unlike me, who generally flitted from face to random face, he catalogued everyone around him, painstakingly, one at a time. He had a singular expression—not angry, not overwhelmed, more markedly concentrated. Not a particularly attractive man, with a wide yet sculpted face and eyes set so far apart it made their lance-like focus inevitably halting, almost aggressive. For a moment I was alarmed that he somehow thought he recognized me, maybe from Wabigoon—one of the men in Lars's store who knew I had gone missing, or maybe a bounty hunter for Pinkerton. His clothing worn and backwoods-like, his hat wider than those worn by the cowboys around him, he gripped a rifle in both hands as though he expected someone to try and take it from him. Defiant. That is the word I am looking for. In any case, once he had committed my face to memory, he moved on to another.

—Hey!

Jake called out to me over the rump of Annie's horse.

—Do you know who that was you were just lookin' at?

I shook my head.

—Gabriel Dumont. He's where you're from. He led some big rebellion.

I glanced over to Dumont once more, this time with the recalibrated sight that context gives. Since he was looking at the crowd on the other side of the street now, I took the chance to take in his figure as a whole. He was top-heavy, built for the strong-arm work he would need to do on a horse, whether charging into a herd of buffalo or harassing Middleton's soldiers. He looked like he knew what he thought and was prepared to act on it. I could practically hear the creaking leather of his saddle and the sound of his horse crunching through prairie snow, even smell the earthy scent of animal hide mingled with gunpowder in his jacket. He had a name for his rifle: Le Petit. I was surprised that Gabriel Dumont was here. From all that I had read about him, I was not surprised that he looked exactly as he did.

Cody's show divided the story of the Indians into two stages: An Enemy in '76; A Friend in '85. This characterization doubled as code for US Indians threatening to win in '76 and finally being vanquished in '85. Spectators saw the fights—likely what they came to see—but incidentally they also saw displays of whites and Indians living together in peace. The Indian women had the bigger reason for complaint, as far as I was concerned, since they appeared in the limited roles of torturers-of-white-women or adjuncts to their men.

By the time the parade wound back down toward the ferry dock, Annie's wave collapsed into a slump just before she listed over, finally giving in to a free fall from her horse, much like the Pinkerton had done. Anticipating her deterioration, I slipped off my horse in time to catch her at the waist. A gentle pull at her belt slid her gracefully down the side of her horse and into my arms, unconscious. Once people around me figured out what had happened, up went a great hue and cry. Jake appeared beside me, along with Cody and others. We made her a makeshift stretcher out of a blanket, which we carried onto the ferry, the train, and finally to her tent, where doctors quickly assembled.

Not knowing what was expected of me once the flap of her tent dropped, I returned to my quarters for no more than an hour before Jake came to find me.

—Come now. They want you in her tent, he whispered.

When I got there, a grave doctor ushered me in. There were others in the tent, and all voices were hushed. The doctor singled me out.

—How did you know to assist Miss Oakley when you did? I am told you were the one to catch her when she slid off her horse.

—I nursed my father through consumption, I answered. I can tell when someone is failing.

He nodded.

—I want you to sit beside her bed. Her ear has been lanced and will bleed for several hours yet. You must keep changing the bandages and at the same time apply cold compresses to her forehead to keep her temperature down.

It was dusk by this time. Darkness was claiming the inside of the tent, except for the candle he had someone light to accompany me in my vigil.

—We believe her to have blood poisoning, he murmured as I sat down. It might be strong enough to claim her. Our only hope is in time and assiduous care.

I looked down at her figure, so vulnerable with that huge dressing on her ear. The doctor continued in a hushed tone.

—If her breathing becomes laboured, or there is any change in her condition, send for me immediately, no matter what the time of night.

I stayed by her side until morning, when the doctor returned and told me to get some sleep because I would probably be required again by nightfall.

I tended to Annie for four nights without her so much as batting an eyelash. Although she was still breathing, the doctor thought she remained hovering at the brink of a decisive turn. A body cannot lay motionless for so long without some sort of consequence. As I draped compresses over her forehead in the deep of night, the irony was not lost on me that I was nursing yet again. Nursing and teaching, nursing and teaching. All that had changed was that this time I was nursing a woman. I pondered whether I had come all this way on January's instructions just to see her die.

At the moment the sun broke on the fifth day, the doctor arrived to relieve me. He told me later that only moments after I left, Annie Oakley opened her eyes and asked hoarsely where her husband was. In the cot beside her, Frank awoke to his prayers answered, prompting much celebration throughout the day. Impossibly, this afternoon Annie performed in the show against the doctor's orders. She was weak, with her ear heavily bandaged, and had to lean on the table to shoot. And yet she dazzled the crowd with her dead-accurate shot. I had never seen anyone like her.

I was so busy during the day that I fell into sleep at night with no apprehension of collapsing onto my cot. Abe and Pinkerton threw themselves enthusiastically into the skits for which they were extras. As Pony Express horses, their penultimate scene was the Deadwood Siege. On their first surge out from behind the backdrop, they carried hooting Indians around the stage. Eventually, each attacker jumped from his horse onto the careening stagecoach. Then, the horses circled around back to the barn, where they picked up the cowboys, who charged out to the front again and saved the day. Judging from Abe's reaction, the horses interpreted all this thundering about as proof they were exceedingly important. Jake said Abe was smart enough to be a trick pony. He was going to start training him the next week. I braced myself for how big that horse's head would be when he was one of the stars.

INSPIRED

After her first few whirlwind days of performing against all odds, Annie Oakley sent for me. She wanted to express her gratitude with a personally prepared breakfast. Jake delivered the message, reporting that Annie mentioned she was anxious to see the face of her guardian angel.

When I arrived at her tent, her husband, Frank, shook my hand for an extended period, even cupping it with his other hand as he did so. He was a warm man, obviously ardently concerned about his wife. With a flourish, he accompanied me to the outside space where Annie, her back to me, fussed with the fire. Frank announced my presence, prompting her to look quickly over her shoulder, and then point to the chair for me to sit down.

—It is a pleasure to arrange the fire just so, she said with her back to me still, as though we had known each other a long time and our habit was to sit here talking casually together. She glanced back at me to add that it was one of those simple tasks that became all important when you could not do them.

I watched as she carefully placed a wire mesh over the fire to hold the small cast-iron frying pan for the bacon, eggs, and steak. Once things were sizzling away to beat the band, as she called it, she turned around to inspect me.

—You're wearing pants, she declared.

Evidently I should have said something to explain, but I was frankly too stunned to answer.

—I do not like women in pants. No matter. Pants or no pants, you helped save my life.

I was given to assume she had dispensed me a favour.

As she slid the contents of her frying pan onto our plates, she recalled the morning when her fever must have broken, when she opened her eyes to hear her Frank whoop and then cry. She did not know before that point how fully he had succumbed to the fear she was lost forever. It was the doctor who told her a British girl caught her from her horse and watched over her through the four nights of her fever.

—I never learned your name. Even the doctor did not know it.

—Abigail.

—You are a recent immigrant?

—To Canada first and now to America.

—My doctor tells me you nursed me every night since the parade.

—I did.

—That must have been exhausting.

—I admire you, Miss Oakley.

She seemed touched by my forthrightness.

—Do you shoot? she asked.

—I am a teacher by vocation but would prefer to shoot. At present I am fully taken up with shovelling manure.

—Hence the men's trousers?

—Hence the men's trousers.

She had an infectious smile.

—You have a horse?

—Two. I have done some practise shooting but have had little chance to shoot while riding.

I watched her cut her steak into small squares of the same dimension.

—Women should know how to shoot, and you have proved yourself deserving. For taking care of me, I would like to reward you with shooting lessons.

She went on to describe how she intended to introduce a new kind of motion to her act with the help of a bicycle, a new invention that intrigued her. Also, she planned to throw her hat in the air and, when it landed on the ground, thunder by on her horse, dangle from the saddle, and pick it up while shooting twenty or so glass balls in the process. She had an idea that on Independence Day she could have the balls filled with red, white, and blue streamers so that her hail of bullets produced a display on the order of fireworks.

She insisted she was not and never had been competitive with the Colonel—she still thought the world of him to this day—but she was not content to let him remain the one and only performer to shoot while galloping on a horse. To make up for undermining his billing as the show's only mounted sharpshooter, she began introducing him as the world's most charming sharpshooter. To that the crowd always burst forth with applause and laughter.

—I need someone to manage the glass balls for me and hand me my guns at the right times. Frank would appreciate the chance to be freed up to do other things. I might be able to squeeze Cody to give you a raise for these new duties.

She was known for chiding Cody to add more women shooters and riders to the show. Now she would tell him she was preparing me as a shooter who would help keep the show's decorum ladylike.

—I would be delighted, raise or not, I said. It would be nothing short of an honour.

She nodded as though one item was now checked off her list, and jumped up to rescue the bubbling coffee pot.

—It is in shooting, not reading and writing, where my gifts lie, but I have always appreciated an educated person. Why have you left teaching?

—I want to become something I have never been, I answered.

—You aren't satisfied with who you are?

—Who I am has changed.

—That sounds odd to me. I have never changed. Quite the contrary, I generally have to fight to go on being who I am.

The following week she invited me to accompany her to The New York Ladies Riding Club, which had not long before awarded her what she described as a lovely gold medal. In return, she generously promised to give shooting lessons at the club for free whenever she was in their vicinity.

—There are always people who want to learn how to shoot, she advised me. Most will tell you they are dedicating themselves to a new skill, when what they really want to do is dress up like a cowboy and randomly shoot whatever will not shoot back.

You could be truly powerful without focus and discipline. Shooting properly meant the ability to act by extending yourself beyond the limits of your person. Shooting was not the capacity to do indiscriminate damage. It was the finesse to be precise with your own moral authority, to choose your own life, defend yourself, and feed yourself if necessary. Both men and women clamoured for shooting lessons. As we rode together, I came to understand that she felt it her role to train me with an assortment of her opinions.

—I do not like Lillian Smith, she told me.

—I have heard that.

—So they talk about it, do they, in the stables and the yards?

—They do.

She grew truly animated on the topic of grammar, and Lillian Smith's use of it was patently unforgivable. According to Annie, this rival shooter had become what the polite called ample, and had always spoken too loudly and too much.

—I do not think women need to be friendly with each other simply because they are women. Women shooters in these rodeo shows are, by and large, unforgivably crass. They act like men and give women a bad reputation. If women begin to act like men, who will act like women? Make no mistake, if we think there should be no difference maintained, women will wind up indistinguishable from men sooner or later, and the world is a bad enough place as it is.

She had no doubt shared all these views with Frank, whom she credited with being the writer of the family. Characterizing him as always scribbling down notes of dates and places and times and names, she was sure they would come in handy if you had a court case to prove. Undoubtedly she thought him a smart man. Everyone in the stables knew the story of how they met. He had entered himself in a shooting match, and was soon disappointed to learn a young woman was the only other contestant in the competition. Not one to let discomfiture ruin his chance to make a little money—even if it did seem to him akin to shooting goldfish in a barrel—he met her on the field. She often said she could tell he was a perfect gentleman because he intended to crush her as a competitor. Any other man could never have fallen in love with a woman who proved she could beat him at a man's game, but her Frank did.

—You think men and women are really so different? I asked.

—A woman can do anything she wishes, but she will never be a man. Men have something stamped into them.

—What is that?

—When it is not plain stupidity, it is a short wire to action.

Was that not what I had been berating myself about all the way from England to here? I thought of my propensity to act as simple impulsiveness, and it inescapably seemed to cost me. I could not divine why that would be any different for a man. Father regretted our lunge into action just as much as I did. Action set things in motion, and the repercussions were not always what you had anticipated or could control. Annie knew that. She made her living as a woman of action.

—What is a woman, then?

—A woman is a more complicated creature. It's why men are better off when they listen to women.

—Surely women cannot be right all the time.

—Complicated does not mean right. Look at those suffragettes. Politics bring nothing but corruption and vice. Women should tend to the more important business of their families.

—Surely you agree that women should vote?

—Do you think men will be nicer to women because they vote? I'll tell you what will make men nicer to women. A man will respect a woman who can shoot him. Guns are the great equalizer.

—But they cause so much damage.

—Your Canadian countrymen used guns to take back the west from Riel. What would you do if your Yankee friends tried to take you over tomorrow?

—Britain would likely intercede.

—And are you somehow more civilized because someone else is willing to do your fighting for you?

—Sitting Bull thinks Americans are evil because of what they have done with their guns.

—And I happen to think Americans were evil in the way they went about things with the Indians. But Americans are capable of righting their wrongs, as we did in Lincoln's war. When you see something worth fighting for, Abigail, I hope you have a gun in your hands.

She was remarkably accepting of my questions, considering the vehemence of her positions. Prone to quoting Mark Twain, she offered, "Loyalty to country *always*. Loyalty to government when it deserves it." In her estimation, Mark Twain was her country's greatest author. He had been known to announce that Annie Oakley "could hit anything with a gun that anyone else could, and then some," which reinforced her contention that he was blessed with the ability to see through liars and bullies to the truth.

When we got to the riding club, Annie lined me up with twenty other women, each one of us aflame with the certitude that we were in the presence of greatness.

As she demonstrated, she exhorted us to think of our rifle as an extension of our eyes and arms.

—The instant of squeezing the trigger must be one of dead calm. You should be perfectly still with a straight back because correct posture prepares for an easy swing of the rifle up to the shoulder. All one movement combines the mind and nerve together.

To my surprise, she pointed me out as an example because I had closed my eyes when I brought my rifle up to my shoulder, which to her was a sign of full commitment.

—Abigail, I invite you to join up for the regiment of women sharpshooters I plan to train and offer to the president of these United States of America, should the need arise here or anywhere else in the world where we are in peril. Women do not need to be passive agents in the defence of their country. We all came to this continent to build a society of free individuals and develop ourselves as the greatest civilization on Earth.

Later I asked if she thought she was born with her gift for shooting, or if it was the result of her own will through practise and determination. She answered immediately that there was no doubt in her mind that she was born with it, a response that deflated me to the point that she regretted giving it to me so quickly and without considering its consequence.

—We are who we are from birth, she explained. We can fail ourselves by not doing the most with what we have, but we cannot turn ourselves into something we are not. Some try mulishly all their lives to be great, only to discover the impossibility of it. We are not all equal in talent, nor anything else for that matter, and yet each one of us has the responsibility to be the best of what we are.

She seemed disturbed by the idea that I felt I had changed into someone I was not before, and told me she hoped I was sure who I was this time. I needed to get on with fully developing myself, whoever I was, over the long haul.

As critical as she was of that which she disapproved, like the Lillian Smiths of the world, she was effusive about what she deemed the good. She showered praise on me for nursing her back from what she was convinced was the edge of her own demise. I heard her recount to many already that, in her delirium, she mistook sliding off her horse into my arms for slipping down a riverbank into water where faces floated out from foliage and sunken logs to leer at her—bloated, grotesque faces she barely remembered. Beasts swam so close to her face that the whoosh of their passing brought drowned noises of grunting and snorting and chewing and swallowing. She had no rifle to take up for protection. Under water, her legs could not run.

She was convinced that what kept her from drowning in this watery hell was a benevolent energy close by, helping her. Someone outside the water, real and trustworthy. She could not determine whether she came to this conclusion as a result of specific words spoken or actions taken. Trapped deep in her mind by the fever, she could not open her eyes or speak to invite this force in to help her do battle with the demons ever tightening their grips. All she knew was that this force stood with her through her darkest hours.

When she heard religious types describing the will of God moving in mysterious ways, she generally believed that, if it was mysterious, something needed to be done about it. Either something fishy was going on, or you were half out of your mind. Even though her mother was a Quaker, Annie was never religious herself and did not know how to compare what she felt to what religious folks felt. She just knew that during this illness a presence guided her when she was confused beyond the ability to tell which way was up. Munificently, she identified that presence as me.

Annie practised every afternoon for two riding stunts, the first shooting two dozen glass balls while riding a bicycle. Despite the inescapable fact that her skirt could trip her up and present a real danger, she refused to wear anything else, more the Victorian lady than anyone I ever met back in England. It was quite a sight to see her all prim and proper perched on her bike with her skirt over her knees, blasting everything that dared fly over her. There was a metaphor for womanhood in there somewhere, although I was at pains to articulate what it might be.

The second stunt was launched from her horse, while she actually reclined on its back and shot the balls pitched above her. She was so diminutive that she could extend her full length on the horse's back. Even Cody, who took credit for the shooting-while-riding stunts, was impressed. Her third and final trick for the summer was to shoot while standing up straight on the back of her horse. She shot birdshot out of her smoothbore gun because Cody once used regular bullets for the task and broke windows blocks away.

As exciting as this new life was, I had not outrun my demons. I still thought of Father every day. I carried forward guilty pangs about running away so ungraciously from Lars and the Swedes. I was also excruciatingly aware that my problem of reporting the Pinkerton crouched in the weeds of my future. In my contented moments, when I was shooting with Annie, managing the horses, or releasing the trap, I caught myself remembering what I had yet to do. Perhaps because I was otherwise so happy, these intruding thoughts of what awaited me wreaked havoc with my nervous system, veritably turning me inside out. It was not long ago that my misery swamped even a fleeting glimpse of happiness. Now, despite being haunted by gnawing moments of trouble yet to come, I was no longer lonely.

By the time I was hired on by the Cody show, Annie and Frank were already well established in their custom of inviting interesting personalities to their tent for evenings of social conversation. On these occasions, she claimed to be making things "right homey" with a deep red plush rug, chintz curtains, and a steamer trunk she used as a table for refreshments. Frank tried some interior decorating of his own, setting out a display of her special awards—guns, jewellery, homemade quilts given to her by people visiting from all over the world and all walks of life, from regular people to princes and kings who appreciated a well-formed shot.

On the road with the show, the couple made train travel as comfortable as possible. Since sleeping while sitting up always left a crick in the neck, they brought boards to place over the seats for makeshift beds that delivered them to their destination feeling fit and ready to go. Despite the vagabond life, their grand tent was a sophisticated place where they could fully embrace the pomp and ceremony of fine living. Exceptional people came to call and tell them about themselves and their work.

Annie invited me to a special evening she was about to host, maintaining I would be interested in it because I hailed from the north. Knowing how she felt about pants, I pulled out my lavender dress from Winnipeg to please her with a ladylike appearance. Good thing I did, considering the jackets and gowns that filled up her tent. With its walls rolled up, the giant tent sparkled with the glory of a natural ballroom, allowing guests to spill outside with their drinks under the stars.

Widely appreciated as a magnanimous hostess, Annie called for everyone's attention, and nodded to the warm applause offered up to her. Anyone could see the joy that flowed through her in the spotlight. She lit up, her face both beautiful and strong, irradiated as though redirecting the crowd's generosity back out to them. She began by recollecting the previous summer, when she and Frank were granted the good fortune of hosting Sitting Bull. He was the saddest man she had ever seen when he talked about getting far enough away from trouble after Little Big Horn to be safe from Americans. Although he temporarily found that place in Canada, he ultimately faced the more formidable enemy of starvation. He could not draw enough nurturance from ground or government to sustain the rest of his people.

—He was the one to name me Little Sureshot and adopt me as his daughter. That is saying something, considering what he thought of Americans. We must insist on acknowledging courage and commitment wherever it is found. Otherwise, how are we to be a heroic people? My new guest for tonight's evening reminds me of Sitting Bull in some ways. He is the sharpshooter from Canada, Gabriel Dumont, also with sad eyes. Both men were generals for their people, one Indian, the other a combination of white and Indian; one American and one Canadian, whether or not they wanted these new nationalities that now draw new borders through their respective nations. Both resisted the unstoppable steam engine and all it brought through their lands. Their courage is all the more impressive because they were vastly outnumbered.

—Sitting Bull told me he participated in so many lost causes that the outcome did not matter as much as the fact that he had fought. I see similar determination in Mr. Dumont, who was also injured in battle. Sitting Bull was shot through the hip and back; Dumont withstood a bullet at Duck Lake that grazed the top of his head. For a long time afterward, he fainted each time he turned his head suddenly. In my opinion, Gabriel Dumont has earned the billing of my equal as the best sharpshooter in the Cody show. I have extended this honour to no one else, including Cody.

Once the translator finished with her words, Dumont nodded acceptance of the compliments she had bestowed upon him. When he began to talk about Saskatchewan, his words rumbled through the deep registers of his timbre and up into the higher pitch of the interpreter who decoded his French. Dumont said what he regretted about the rebellion was the fact it had accomplished nothing. He wanted reparations for his Métis fighters. He wanted to see them back on their farms now that the battle was over, and he intended to keep speaking to people about their rebellion until that happened.

As he spoke about his battles, my mind drifted to the American founders of this new country. Had they not won their rebellion, they would have been fugitives just like Dumont, hoping to outsmart British bounty hunters long enough to die natural deaths. Although there was no telling if an amnesty would have been offered to the writers of the American Constitution, British rulers had never been known for their compassion.

As soon as he indicated he would entertain questions from the audience, a man asked him to explain the problem he had with land claims. Dumont answered that many Métis had been on their land for four years without having their claims processed into deeds by the government, which meant they were losing out on their second homestead privilege. This meant that settlers who had their titles processed in time to claim a second homestead could do so right out from under Métis neighbours who were still waiting. On a couple of occasions, the Métis had been driven to attach ropes to their horse saddles and pull down outbuildings someone else had raised to stake ownership.

—Surely you didn't go to war simply because of a bureaucratic delay, one woman piped up.

From Annie's scowl, I deduced the woman was a journalist. Dumont's eyes could bore through granite.

—My friend Louis Riel was right when he said that we Métis suddenly live in a world we do not understand, one where we do not belong.

—You still have to survive, the woman countered.

—There were sixty million buffalo only a few years ago. No one imagined they could disappear. We hoped this reality would change. It has not.

—If you knew then what you know now, asked another, if you had the chance again to decide whether you would take up arms and rebel, would you do it?

His face was fiercely set, his voice deep.

—I spent four days after the battle looking for Riel. Each night I camped right in Batoche, and each day I tracked the patrols sent out to look for me. They never thought to look back over their shoulders. Middleton looted and burned our houses, drove off our livestock, and torched what few crops we had scratched out of the hard prairie soil. Whenever Middleton saw those of mixed blood, whether they had ever participated in the rebellion or not, he took over their property. We made our choice as warriors. We will live with the consequences.

After Dumont's speech, Annie linked arms with a young man who had been standing close by her. He struck me as close to her age, and remarkably handsome with his trimmed beard and snappy brown suit. He and Frank laughed at something Annie said, and I remarked to myself that they seemed easy with each other, like family. Perhaps he was Annie's brother. I expected her to mingle with her more distinguished guests, but she made a beeline for me.

—This is Shea Wyatt, Abigail. He redeems journalism by writing exclusively and accurately about me whenever I am in town. While I am not in the city, he amuses himself with the law. Shea, this is Abigail, just in from Canada, who has already become dear to me.

Ordinarily I simply would have flushed under the appreciative look of so good-looking a young man. Instead, I descended into an apoplectic episode. From my feeling of sudden disequilibrium and their looks of alarm, I could tell the colour of my face had drained to the glazed white of porcelain.

—Please forgive me, I said. I am quite overwhelmed. I never expected to be standing in a room with Gabriel Dumont. I am pleased to meet you, Mr. Wyatt.

Shea and Annie laughed, thinking me star-struck, as I desperately fought to regain control of myself upon the shock of so suddenly finding the man I had come all this way to find. It seemed impossible to me that these two people could have had anything to do with Shep January.

Wyatt was obviously sufficiently close to Annie to be familiar with the phenomenon of ladies flocking to Annie from her gun clubs. We were all quite accustomed to those legions of female fans looking to Annie for leadership in this new land. It was the norm for people to gush in her presence, to flounder through questions and exclaim their admiration. She was always the star of the show. But I had the impression he registered that it was not Annie or Dumont who so flummoxed me, but rather himself.

Perhaps as a way to finesse my story of why I was here, he offered an explanation for his own presence at this function.

—Annie and I did not attend much school as children, and so we appreciate the oppressiveness of ignorance. She now imports experts because she is hungry to know everything: how skyscrapers might be built, how diseases rage and medicines protect, how a philosophy might change the world or a political theory might improve people's lives. Annie has invited me to come and write about your compatriot Mr. Dumont.

—I imagine he would think me more enemy than compatriot, but I do agree he is worth writing about.

—How so? he asked, his eyes now trained on me.

He and Annie had a way of making their interest clear when

something piqued it. This habit seemed part of a widespread American propensity for frankness. The British were more circumspect about what interested them, as though something were to be given away should they admit intrigue. Americans seemed to celebrate it. I could not tell if he was suspicious of me. I found myself caught between the two dispositions.

—I admire his willingness to act when something matters to him, I said.

—Even when it ends in defeat?

—From what I understand, it might have turned out otherwise. I have read that he allowed Mr. Riel to channel bad military advice from God. I believe that Dumont, if left unbridled, might have put his talent for ambush to more successful use. Macdonald could not have suffered a true threat to his railroad just before the last spike.

His thoughtful half-smile made me think he must have some British running through his veins.

—But who am I to know, I followed up quickly. I certainly was not there to assess the situation.

—Do you understand the issues of land scrips that Mr. Dumont raises?

—Only what I learned in Canadian newspapers as I followed the rebellion.

—I would like to write an article about Mr. Dumont and his rebellion. Could I trouble you to drop by my office the next time you are in Manhattan? You could get me started on my research with what you know of the Canadian experience and attitude about the rebellion.

I feared I might have been too obvious in my enthusiasm as I practically grabbed the business card out of his hand. Annie flashed what I interpreted as a subtle look of curiosity, and I faltered at the thought that she would judge me as being forward. She would not like that, but apparently granting me the benefit of the doubt, she seemed to accept that a dramatic response was to be expected upon exposure to her charming young man. I tried nodding more demurely as I slipped his card into the sleeve of my dress.

Whether either one of them was suspicious of me, they could not possibly have distinguished the movement of tectonic plates beneath all four of us—Abigail, Shea, Dumont, and myself. Here in this tent, on this night, and without knowing it, I had set forces in motion.

I could not stand the possibility of them feeling betrayed by me. Even if only Wyatt had noticed my reaction to his name, his mention of it to Annie could undo the friendliness she bestowed upon me every day. A guardian angel did not sneak up on a person.

And so, at the end of the night, I kept Annie and Frank up all hours with my wild and improbable story. They hardly knew what to make of it. The detail most difficult for them to comprehend was the possibility of my having shot and killed a Pinkerton detective! Even granting a measure of natural talent, Annie said she would never have wagered on me in a shootout. By morning she said she was seeing a more iron-fisted side of me because I could not be shaken from my conviction that Shea would turn in my guns and clear up the incident with the Pinkerton. She called it conviction, but I knew it as desperation. I was all in now, and January had given me to believe that all I had to do was find them. Now I had told Annie my entire story, and neither of them had ever heard of him or known anything of him.

EXPOSED

I dragged Annie to Wyatt's office the next morning, risking her disapprobation in my fringed jacket and men's trousers. I was bringing them the gritty truth, and might as well look the part. Besides, I was no longer a teacher. I looked like someone who did what I actually did each day. And yet, all the way over on the ferry, she remained oblivious to the trousers, as though she had not even noticed. Wyatt was the one with the reaction, a look of alarm at seeing me so different. Last night, my lilac dress matched my British accent. Today, I looked more like Lillian Smith or Calamity Jane pounding at his door. I could see him struggle to square his first impressions of me with my present appearance as a character out of a dime store novel.

Annie sat down on the settee at my back as I perched myself on the chair in front of Wyatt, who faced me from behind his large mahogany desk. He may well have heard many a tale from this chair, but mine would vie for the prize. Annie remained silent as she listened. I watched his eyes narrow and widen by turns as he processed all I told him. He could accept the immigrant experience as excruciating, the loss of a father debilitating. He could imagine a stranger coming to town and even accord me the attraction of going on a journey. What he could not understand, and returned to over and over despite my growing exasperation with its repetition, was my motivation to travel alone, through dangerous territory, all the way to New York. ·

—To do the right thing, I cried.

—You could have done the right thing by taking your story to the North-West Mounted Police after your father died.

—They still would have had to get these guns to the Pinkerton Company. If I had left it for them to do, they might have put me in jail.

—You could have taken the train from Wabigoon to New York, bought horses there, and found the job you now have. Why the convoluted and dangerous route?

—In a town so small as Wabigoon, you cannot just get on a train without it becoming everyone's news. I wanted to slip away without having to explain myself. There was too much to explain.

—You could have left well enough alone and not told anyone about the Pinkerton. It might be several lifetimes before anyone discovered your secret.

—I killed and buried a man! I cannot live with myself without owning up to the catastrophe and letting his family know what happened.

—What if I present your affidavit and they arrest you?

—You would defend me, would you not? Surely the truth would win out.

—It would be your word against all kinds of reasons not to believe you.

—But you believe me?

138

—Why did January tell you to find me?

—I assumed he knew you were someone to be trusted.

—How would he know that when I have no idea who he is?

—He neglected to tell me you would not know him.

He conceded that I had an obligation to let the Pinkerton's family know what happened to him. Plus, he had to agree that honesty was the best policy in the pursuit of justice, especially if I wanted to press my case that the shooting was an accident. And he could understand I would be in a stronger position if free to work on my case. He knew I was right that the police might very well have held me in a jail cell up north for safekeeping, especially if they corroborated my story by disinterring the Pinkerton.

There are days in many if not all our lives when we make a decision that determines our future in some fundamental way. Even if the episode begins with a stroke of good luck or bad, we make a decision to respond. How many have squandered a windfall, or spurned someone who one day comes back more powerful to avenge the slight? Alternatively, how many have treated good luck as a second chance and turned a broken life into a glorious one? This was such a day for Shea Wyatt. He was a relatively new attorney, and I had a particularly sticky story.

For Annie, there was no hesitation between the apprehension of danger and the hair-trigger solution that dispensed so quickly with clay pigeons and glass balls. To Shea, justice was a product of sober thought and careful analysis. For him, time and patience guarded against the half-cocked gun. He glanced over at Annie.

—It's not like you to be so quiet.

She jumped out of her chair and began to pace.

—I have been beating the cobwebs out of my mind. I think I have a vague recollection of once before noting so unusual a name as January.

She recalled when she and Shea were working together at the Sills Brothers Circus. He must have been nineteen because she was performing in the shooting show and he was helping with the animals. One day a man showed up at her tent asserting that he was there on an urgent matter from a law firm that had something to do with Shea's mother.

—The only reason I allowed him to step inside our tent was the fact that Frank was there with me. That was the man I told you about who claimed that your aunt in England had died with a provision in her will for your mother. With the beneficiary dead, her inheritance would go to her son's generation.

—I assumed he was only a messenger.

—You were out back with the elephants. I offered to call you, but he said he was in a hurry. I remember asking him to repeat who he was, to which he responded "January" from the New York firm Evans and White. I was more interested in getting the firm's name right.

Shea returned to me.

—You aren't the only one to receive money from this mysterious man. When I opened the package, it contained a thousand dollars in cash, and no letter of explanation. Later, after attempting to contact the firm, we discovered there was no firm in New York by that name. Annie, you never told me the man's name before.

—I don't know that I could have recalled it on my own. I recognize it only because you said it, and because it is an odd name. At the time, we were more interested in what you should do with your windfall.

—What *did* you do with it? I asked.

—I arranged an apprenticeship in the law. For the next three years I lived on that money and read myself silly until I qualified for the bar. A spinster aunt in England seemed plausible until I eventually discovered that my two younger brothers had not heard of any inheritance. Why did the man not go to Mr. Sills?

—And how did he know to give the package to me? Annie asked. He must have known about our connection. I am not in the habit of consorting with criminals, not that plenty don't show up in a wild-west show as employee or patron. Sometimes people think they know me just because they saw me shoot, or asked for my autograph. But not every Tom, Dick, and Harry knows you and I go back to the Sills Brothers Circus. Is this a fluke or a plot?

—I have the guns in a safe deposit box at the bank, I said. Let me at least prove that part of my story.

The two of them exchanged a glance I could not read. Annie stood up.

—I have to get back to prepare for my performance.

—We'll walk you down to the ferry, Shea said.

When we reached the docks, Annie turned to me before stepping on the ferry.

—I never would have believed any of this if you hadn't been the one to catch me in my fever. I make up my own mind about people. You may have a hard time convincing Shea, here. But I have made my mind up about you, and that's not going to change.

—Thank you, Annie, I said.

—January was right about one thing. You've got some kind of luck in you.

As we walked the short distance to the bank, I sensed that Wyatt was not persuaded. We were an unlikely pair, he and I, me looking like I should have a shovel in my hands and him the exemplar of a court advocate. As soon as we walked into the bank, the teller waved to me in recognition. I shook his extended hand.

—This is Mr. Wyatt, the other name on my card.

—Ah, he said, and flipped through his drawer of cards until he found it.

—You used my name before you even found me? Wyatt whispered behind me as we followed the clerk down the hall to the first anteroom.

—I was convinced you were the one who would make everything right.

The clerk left us alone in the room for a couple of minutes before returning to thump the box down on the table and close the door behind him. Wyatt took the only seat in the room, off to one side of the table.

—You do not seem anxious for me to open it, I said.

—I thought I'd give you the chance to change your mind.

He twirled a grey cowboy hat in his hands the way some men jingle change in a pocket. With anyone else, I would have thought it a nervous gesture. We both stared at his hat as he spun it.

—This is the moment that has kept me going for the last year, I said.

—Hmm, he said at length. I guess that's a no, then.

And then I laughed.

—Admit it, now, I chided. You would be disappointed if Pandora's box remained closed forever.

—One might say guns are guns, and they inevitably come to no good.

—And then you would miss their individual stories, would you not? I am sure Annie would not agree with you.

He shrugged while I set to work unlocking my demons. I wanted to hand all of it over to him so I might feel the burden lift from my shoulders. As I cranked open the lid, everything was there, exactly as I had left it. It looked like a box full of money. He stood and joined me at the table, exhaling a long, low whistle.

—How did you get all this way without someone taking that from you.

It was more a statement of disbelief than a question. I pulled out the packets of bills and stacked them on the table.

—This is only a third of the money. When the time comes, I will have to figure out how to consolidate it all from Winnipeg and the other New York bank.

I handed him January's gun first. He held it in one hand, perhaps sensing the first indication of a new weight as he inspected it.

—It's in surprisingly good shape for such an old gun. Well oiled.

—We used it in my practise sessions. He wanted to make sure I could defend myself if someone came at me up close.

He nodded as he stared at it before handing it back to me. I traded him for Pinkerton's gun.

—Flashier, he said about the mother-of-pearl handles.

—A gun tells you something about its owner, I think. I refuse to say anything good about January, but I am pretty sure I would have liked Pinkerton even less.

—You have something against fancy guns?

—When they come with a willingness to shoot someone from behind, I do.

He handed me back the gun, but his eyes rested on my face.

—No one would ever know you have all this here. You could walk away and save yourself a world of trouble.

—I know it is here. And now so do you.

I summoned the bank clerk, who picked up the box and left the room. Wyatt and I walked together through the bank to the front door, where the sun blazed down on the bustling street before us. A flutter of panic swept through me. He was still reluctant. January had given me no indication of what might motivate Wyatt to help me. In retrospect, it was stupid of me not to ask about that while I had the chance. I felt sure that this noble stranger seemed uninterested in the money, and unmotivated by a damsel in distress.

—From what you say, January would appreciate the irony of his guns and money winding up in a bank, he said genially.

—It is where I would expect an attorney to put them.

—I think he cased you pretty well. He had enough life left in him to move on if he didn't think you could follow his instructions.

Why had that not occurred to me? I presumed January had no choice because he was dying. He trained me for weeks. He could have made it back down to the US and buried his loot if he had decided against trusting me. He could have made a will with a lawyer in any town. Surely he cared about someone sufficiently to wish them his money.

There was a cold hand of something manipulative at work. If I felt it, Wyatt must have felt it. I could be setting Wyatt up for something I did not even suspect. I would never know.

Wyatt kept looking up at the sun and closing his eyes.

—Care to join me for lunch?

—What?

—I have some things to explain to you.

In the busy saloon, I saw confusion flit over the bartender's face when the man in the suit ordered the shot of whiskey while I, in my leather and fringe, no doubt along with a feint odour of manure, primly ordered the soup and fowl.

—Look, he said. I believe you think you are doing the right thing.

—But?

—I don't think you understand what you could be getting yourself into. You want to fight for the truth, but you don't even know what it is. January could have set a trap for you.

—Why would he do that?

—An old vendetta, a promise. A score he wanted to settle, a point he wanted to make, or joke he wanted to launch from the grave. He has pulled you, me, and Annie into the web of a dead detective, and buried it in money. Doesn't that look suspicious to you? There are jealous people out there who would love to make Annie look bad, people with grudges, people who just like to bring famous people down.

—If I hide this, I look guilty, and I am not guilty.

—Are you prepared to go to jail for life if you can't prove it?

Around us chairs scraped, human voices chattered and laughed. Was a man's death, and my innocence and freedom, all to be so arbitrarily determined? Was I to run away from this business because I could get away with it? I put down my knife and fork on the table.

—Pragmatism is a coward's way out. You start with the truth, and you fight for it. The outcome is not the issue.

He took a sip of his whiskey.

—My legal opinion is that this is too dangerous for you. I have a personal policy never to hear a client say "You didn't tell me this could happen." I'm telling you that you could wind up spending the rest of your life in jail, whether here or extradited back to Canada.

—I know that.

—The other question I must consider is how I can accept a client who refuses to listen to my legal advice.

—I predict that Annie will agree that you should help me.

—Annie isn't a lawyer, and I'm the one who would have to look her in the eye when you go to jail. You have very quickly managed to become important to her.

Somehow, his articulation made her commitment to me more real. That gave Wyatt and me something solid in common.

—How did you two meet? I asked.

We both sat back as a steaming tureen of soup was placed down in front of me, a thick puree of comfort to help me manage what might be the most important conversation of my life. The introduction of food transformed our table from an office desk into his personally provided hospitality. Or maybe it was the introduction of Annie that softened his stance from hard-nosed professional to wistful friend.

—I'll have to go back a bit about her so you can understand the context of how I came into her life, he said. Annie was five when her father was caught in a blizzard. It happened early in the day, while he was delivering grain to the mill, and it took until midnight for him to make it home. By then his hands were frozen, and his voice gone. He lingered through the winter as an invalid, never again to deliver the mail or bring in money to help her mother. He succumbed to pneumonia in the spring. His widow was left penniless with seven children under the age of fifteen. Whenever we talk about this part of her life, Annie quotes Mark Twain: "The world owes you nothing. It was here first."

As I laughed, I tried to identify what it was about the timbre of his voice that touched me so intimately. The magic was not in what he was telling me. The story itself was horrendous. His mellifluous voice put me in mind of opening a window that looked out onto the world, and he was telling me what he saw. I had a sudden conviction that whenever he opened that window, the same landscape would be there, as though he described the bedrock that was evident to me.

It took a couple of hours for him to relate his story about Annie, and I marvelled as he told it that he was willing to share it with me. He had to feel seriously about something to take this time to help me understand what I had walked into. For him to make his decision, something about Annie needed to be clear to me. As he spoke, I tried to decipher if he was telling me all this to let me down more easily.

—Annie was seven when she figured out how to make a trap using cornstalks and string that worked equally well with squirrels, quail, and grouse. Her catches went some way in helping her mother feed all those kids hand to mouth—for a while, anyway. One day she noticed the old cap and ball Kentucky rifle that had hung above their fireplace since her father died, and that was the day she discovered shooting. The first day was remarkable only because she stuffed the gun so full of powder she could have killed a buffalo. Being born with a gift does not mean you know how to use it. Despite her mother's resistance to a firearm because of her religion, Annie refined her shot and eventually made a reputation for herself with locals who purchased game. Her game sold itself because her kills were always clean, shot clear through their tiny heads without any contaminating lead in the body meat.

—Her family kicked furiously to keep their heads above water on a smaller, cash-leased farm. They did housework, canned food, mended clothes, fed the animals, and farmed the land without ever producing enough to provide for themselves. By the time Annie was nine, her exhausted mother was forced to send her children away to different poor farms. The couple who ran the poorhouse where Annie went taught her to knit and sew. They were pious and pleasant, and she thought she just might manage her new circumstances. Until the day she saw evil walk through the front door. The poorhouse couple believed leasing her out to the farmer she would call the he-wolf might benefit her. Annie was to watch a baby for his wife to free up his wife's time to tend to the house and the older children. Annie was to be repaid with a small wage to be sent to her mother, room and board, and the promise of going to school. Her ability to trap and shoot was a welcome benefit, as far as he was concerned. It did not take long before she could see his plan was to work her to death.

—As their prisoner, she was up at four every morning, underfed, forced to milk the cows and skim the milk, cook breakfast, do the dishes, feed the calves and pigs, weed the garden, collect berries, cook dinner, and care for the baby. In between, she was to trap and hunt. One night when she fell asleep while darning socks, the she-wolf slapped her senseless and threw her out in the snow in her bare feet. It was only when the he-wolf could be heard returning home that she yanked the half-frozen girl back in the house to thaw her out. The next morning Annie was consumed by a fever that almost sent her the way of her father.

—She persevered because she thought her fifty cents per week was being sent to her mother, who thought her daughter was going to school. One day, two years after having come to this farm, when the family was gone and Annie was ironing a basket of clothing, it struck her that she could run away. This possibility had quite simply never crossed her mind before. Even though she had a gun and hunted, she never thought of shooting the he-wolf or trekking past the forest and on to where her mother surely must be.

—With scars across her back and no knowledge of how to read or write, she walked in the direction where she had heard the railroad whistle and soon found the station. Once aboard the crowded train, she told the man beside her she had no money for the fare. He paid her way and asked another passenger to put her off the train at the town nearest to her mother. She maintains to this day that she will always feel beholden to that stranger, and regrets never asking his name.

—Although her mother was elated to see her, she could take Annie in for only a short time, since illness and injury still characterized their existence, and the financial prospects had not improved with her new husband. Annie retraced her steps to the couple at the first poor farm, but this time she was a different girl. This time, when the he-wolf came looking for her, she ran into the woods before the couple could give her back to him. The weakness of those well-intentioned believers, who could not identify the evil leering at them, taught her the power to act when no one else would. She went back later and told them she would shoot him before he ever got hold of her again. The day she met me, I was ten and she eleven, although she would not in any other circumstances admit her birth date. Show business people care about such stupid things as age.

I laughed.

—Annie has mentioned several times that human cantaloupes like Lillian Smith would just love to bully their way into the show as the new young shooters who aspire to replace the has-been Annie Oakley.

—Let her try, we said together, quoting Annie, both smiling at the impossibility.

—I would never tell a stranger my age, in case it was used to figure out hers.

—She will be a better shooter at eighty with her eyes closed than Smith will be at any age.

—Annie was eleven years old when she knocked on the door of a hotel where she often sold her game. On an ordinary day, that door would soon be answered by a perfectly reasonable man, the grocer, chef, and owner of the establishment. Many a stranger was no doubt welcomed there with a warm bed and satisfying meal before going on their way to business elsewhere. Annie knew even then that evil did not always have a recognizable look.

—On that day, the grocer did not answer the front door. Instead, a squat woman with wary eyes told her to take the partridges and grouse around to the back. Annie thought nothing of it because she knew that his storeroom, kitchen, and workshop were all located downstairs. He spent most of his time closer to the back door than the front, except for the trips he made upstairs ferrying his bounty to the dining room.

—Nobody answered at the back door. Since the woman had given her to understand he was home, Annie concluded he had not heard her, so she knocked again. Still no answer. She decided to investigate and push the door open, expecting him to be butchering meat or hammering it out at his worktable. The lights were off and the worktable abandoned. She maintains there are different types of silence to distinguish in this world. One is the kind of quiet produced by happy activity—a delicious meal, an engrossing book—no one making noise because there is so much to claim one's concentration. If she was out in a forest where birds and cicadas were quiet, where the only sound came from faint rustlings under the leaves in anticipation of her footfalls, she knew nothing was amiss. The forest was quiet with relaxed life.

—The other type of silence deadens all life around it. It occurs when everyone in the environment detects a danger that no one has the power to confront. The palpable temperature of cold dread is set by the hysterical hope that an oppressive power might remain insensible to its own possibilities. She stood still in the doorway for the longest time, waiting for something to move. Eventually her patience was rewarded with a distant scraping in the direction of the storeroom wall, behind a barrel. She crept slowly toward it to find a boy near her age lying on the floor, with one eye swollen shut and blood from his mouth smeared on his shirt.

—You? I asked.

He nodded.

—Suddenly a voice tore open nearby, roaring his demand to know who it was. Instinctively, Annie dropped down beside me and waited a few moments before stretching around the barrel to see the grocer standing in the open doorway, his miserable face scrunched up in the light. As though he heard a voice from the depths of hell suddenly answer him, he assumed someone was there to fight. Stumbling about the sacks and barrels all around, he punched whatever appeared in his way. She could make no sense of his ramblings as he fell, picked himself up again, and lunged onto the next phantom that needed pummelling. As the grocer hectored his fiend back toward the work area, Annie grabbed my hand. At first I resisted. There is a strange illogic of safety that makes you want to stand stock still.

—I have read about this reaction in dogs that are kicked so often their understanding of escape evaporates. Even with the door to their cage held wide open, they lie still.

He nodded, then shrugged.

—In the clutch of a tyrant, the beaten know their survival depends on bowing down and staying still. That is when evil manifests itself in its full contradiction. Annie says evil makes you believe it is all powerful, makes you forget that, with persistence, the good will win out every time because evil can survive only by feeding on good. Marshalling all her might, she yanked me up to my feet. Pulling me, she was obviously thinking about Mark Twain because she said, "It's not the size of the dog in the fight, it's the size of the fight in the dog." She dragged me out the door, whispering, "Come on, kid. Give me your fight."

—Once my feet started moving, the escape route plunged open before me. As we raced out into the forest, my sinews and nerves reminded my muscles what they could do. Eventually we reached the place she often used as a campsite, both of us gulping air. She let me crumple to the ground and stare vacantly while she built a fire and roasted one of the partridges she still clutched in her other hand. The meat brought me to my senses, and we had ourselves what we called a right enjoyable feast as we plotted how we would manage the tyrant.

—Just before dawn, I sneaked back into the storeroom to curl up on my sleeping pallet near the kitchen stove as though I had never left. The sun peeping over the horizon was Annie's cue to knock loudly at the storeroom door until the grocer finally hauled himself out of the bowels of his nightmare, hair all on end and breath sour. He stood listening, swaying slightly as she chattered charmingly to give him the impression that this was a regular day when he could act as though he had not been a mean and stinking drunk only hours ago. Conspicuously wanting to evade what he had done, he became downright invigorated by the sounds of chairs scraping overhead as his hotel patrons started waking up. Soon they would straggle into his dining room, hungry and anxious to be on their way. Once he paid for her remaining partridge and grouse, he hobbled back to his worktable to wield his butcher knife like a man pursued by the brutes he had so recently chased.

—Had the grocer's malignant disposition endured into the morning, we had worked out a series of codes about what to do next. I wanted to tie him up, but Annie remained firm about the unlikelihood of two children overwhelming a demented adult. She pointed out that we were still indentured. No one was going to listen to the complaints of legal chattel. To her, the backup plan was the better of the two, and had it been needed she would have jumped to that one in a hurry.

—She often says she does not like liars, and dislikes bullies even more. The most potent weapon she ever learned is the understanding that evil enjoys its capacity to paralyze the good. This can happen in lots of ways. For example, it can come as the conclusion drawn by an intelligent creature at the moment he perceives there is no workable way to prevail. In that case, self-preservation dictates that you see reality for what it is early, before the evil becomes bloated with your helplessness. If for some reason Annie and I were unable to control him as he continued his rage, she was going to shoot him. Even though she would aim for his leg or shoulder to slow him down without killing him, she could well have spent the rest of her youth in some form of juvenile jail, despite any plea of constructive self-defence or defence of others. She still asks herself from time to time what Frank would have thought of her had she been both a sharpshooter and a criminal.

—In any case, once the grocer sobered up to the now pounding footsteps upstairs, we were safely over the waterfall. I fell back into my routine of chopping the vegetables, carrying out the garbage, milking the cow, churning the butter, scooping the cream, and cleaning the floors, and she went back to her hunting. This time I had in my head that I was not a prisoner. I was making a trade of work for food until the day I came of age. Although our campsite was outfitted with the three cans of beans we had buried along with an old pot and matches wrapped up to stay dry, living there for any length of time would have presented new problems. Officials would soon start looking for me, animals might prey on me, food would become more difficult to come by over time and, worst of all, I would have nothing to do all day. We agreed it would be best if I could figure out a way to stay with the grocer so long as I was able to protect myself.

—Next time, at the first sign of the grocer's drinking, I was to light out for our secret campsite. Since Annie came every few days with new game, she would check the campsite first. If she found me at our hiding place, we would wait until dawn to rouse the grocer once again to pay for his birds and get busy. Since the man became a drunken monster every couple of weeks, she and I spent many nights out at our campfire telling each other stories and putting our heads together to plan for the days to come when we were old enough to be our own masters. I wanted nothing more than to step into my dead father's boots as a sheriff.

When Shea finished his story, I felt as though I had been in a trance for hours. Darkness had infiltrated Manhattan outside the saloon, where the new electric arc lamp now jumped to life, reclaiming its own circle of light. Inside, old gas lamps flickered shadows over Wyatt's face as he drained his whiskey.

—Do you know why I have told you all this? he asked.

—I think so.

He raised his eyebrows.

—You are telling me you will take my case.

It was the first time I heard him laugh.

—And how have you deduced that?

—Annie helped to save you, and I helped save Annie. You cannot stand the thought of letting her down.

—Astute.

I pressed my hands down on the table.

—I am beginning to see that January actually did know what he was doing, I said.

He stared at my fingers as though waiting for them to give him a sign.

—Let's just hope he doesn't have anything else waiting to snare us, he answered.

I reached into my pants pocket and withdrew my second key for the safe deposit box. Placing it on the table between us, I pushed it toward him. He let it sit there for a moment, then picked it up and put it in the inside breast pocket of his jacket.

Late in the summer, we moved Bill Cody's newly revamped Wild West show from Staten Island across the river to Manhattan for an additional three-month run. The show began with primeval forests stretching their stick arms over the Dawn of Civilization in the first act, and then proceeded over four more acts to span the existence of the world itself, up to the climax of the American Frontier. By the time Cody's workers had finished banging together the backdrop of trees and cacti in Madison Square Garden, the show stretched three blocks north of Fifth Avenue and Broadway, complete with a blower for the convincingly terrifying cyclone.

I embraced every opportunity Annie made possible for me to work on her rodeo shooting, whether it was to ride to gun clubs and special tournaments or to simply come out to the arena and release pigeons for her. One day Shea accompanied us to the New York Ladies Gun Club, where Annie had organized a shooting competition for beginners. Annie conscripted him to help with the clay pigeon trap, since I would be taken up with helping her position the women properly in their stances. After a morning of dozens of women standing off with targets set up in a field, a whistle blew for lunch at the clubhouse. That was when I appeared in front of Shea with yet another request.

—I am dying to practise shooting while riding a horse. Would you ride beside me and throw things up in the air for me to shoot?

—There is nothing I would love more. And, he said with a smile, I have discovered you are a difficult person to refuse.

—That is about the most marvellous answer you could have given.

—Then I suppose I'm obliged.

I brought Abe and Pinkerton to the grounds, ostensibly to give them both exercise, but I had concocted my plan before we ever started the day's contest. I had it all figured out, where we could ride in a pasture owned by the club that was far enough away not to present safety concerns.

—You can take Abe, I said. He is the smarter horse and will figure out what you are doing more quickly. You can ride out ahead of me and lob these glass balls up as high as you can.

—And you'll be galloping behind me hoping to shoot them without shooting me?

—If you get them high enough, I can avoid such a mistake. I only shoot men who demonstrate a willingness to shoot me in the back.

He laughed outright.

—I missed that connection, but now that you point it out—

—Really, Shea. I would have to shoot you on purpose to make that big of a mistake.

Once he was on the horse, I handed up the big basket of clay pigeons and glass balls, and he followed me out to the pasture. At first we were both awkward, him with throwing more horizontally than vertically, and me shooting wide, over-compensating to make sure he was nowhere near my line of fire. After a bit of practise, he threw a glass ball high enough for me to blast open the red, white, and blue streamers and delight in watching them float down exultantly overhead. Flushed and exhilarated, I galloped past him and stuck out my hand in a victory salute as though having defeated Napoleon himself.

Soon we were racing side by side in a wide circle so he could whip the target into the centre, and I had to track its shift from in front to behind us, with him out of the way. Each time, he threw it somewhere unexpected, which inspired me as a real-life situation instead of the predictability of a pull machine. He had a ball in one hand and a clay pigeon ready to toss simultaneously from the other, when Abe stopped dead in his tracks. Shea sailed over Abe's head into a copse of swampy grass. My shriek must have been the last thing he heard before hitting the ground.

A deluge of memories stormed through my mind, snippets of dead men's faces, shovelfuls of dirt and rock for their graves, all the bits adding up to my losses. Instantly convinced this was to be another dead man for me, I was at his side in an instant, frantically checking him for injuries.

—I'm all right, he said.

I must have heard his words, but something in me refused to

believe them. I kept checking each arm and leg compulsively before bursting into tears.

—Hey, he said. I am not injured. The ground is soft here. A bit wet is all.

I sat with my head on my knees, sobbing. He put his arm around me in comfort, to which I responded by melting into him. Knowing my distress had raced out beyond the immediate circumstance, he kissed me. He wrapped his arms around me until well after my sobbing had stopped.

Suddenly, I furiously pushed myself back to my feet. With fists on my hips, I faced off in front of Abe.

—You will *never* do that again, I yelled at him.

He jerked his head back, as though arguing with me. To that, I turned around to give him my back. He nudged one shoulder with his nose without response. When he nudged my other shoulder, I folded my arms over my chest and stayed put. In short order, he came back to me, sat down, and offered his front leg, as Jake had taught him to do as a trick pony.

—Get on him, I called as I ran toward Shea. He is apologizing to you.

Shea wheeled his leg up over the saddle and hauled me up to sit behind him. I slid my arms around his waist, hugged him tight, and buried my face in his back as we trotted back toward the clubhouse. Pinkerton followed behind without anyone holding his reins. We did not talk about the incident again. I knew from that day Abe would never cause me trouble again, and that Shea was in love with me, as I was with him.

CORNERED

We spent the fall of 1886 and into the winter of '87 debating how best to present my case to the authorities. I wanted to rush into it, on the argument that the Pinkerton's family had a right to know what happened as soon as possible. To Shea, the more facts we could compile to corroborate my story, the more likely the authorities would believe I was telling the truth. The ownership of the Pinkerton gun was probably the easiest to confirm. January's gun would be more difficult. At some point, the North-West Mounted Police would have to dig up both bodies.

Until he had a chance to complete his preparation for my case, Shea wanted to take the precaution of getting me out of the way. In all likelihood, there would be fallout after he submitted his report to the Pinkertons and the police. That was why he recommended I go along to England in Cody's show. Anyone looking to overreact would just have to hold his horses for a few months. Shea could then orchestrate a disclosure meeting and give us some control over the conditions. He could point out that I was coming back willingly to give information so that justice could be done. What kind of murderer would make it safely beyond the arm of the law and still come back for a voluntary chat? He would be sure to make this point. If they did not agree, we still had some room to manoeuvre regarding what I might do and when.

And so, on March 31, 1887, Annie, Frank, and I boarded the steamship *State of Nebraska* at the docks of New York City. Cody loved grand titles, and Queen Victoria's Jubilee sounded like an exotic dessert. We were taking the story of our American West to a place where most people knew at least one family member who had gone to the New World. Cody flung himself into the task of showing these old relations what they had missed. I tagged along with those who were proud to be the first society formed on the principle that there was no need for rulers. "By the people and for the people" was practically an incantation, I heard it repeated so often. The United States was coming back to the mother country, not as a dutiful child, but as a free and equal cousin. We would tell my old compatriots the greatest frontier story in history.

I thrilled at the scale of this enterprise. In addition to scores of shooters and various kinds of performers, a thirty-six-piece band, and stage hands, there were almost a hundred Indians, including Black Elk, the popular and devastatingly good-looking Red Shirt, Mr. and Mrs. Walking Buffalo, Mr. and Mrs. Eagle Horse, Moccasin Tom, Blue Rainbow, Iron Good Voice, Mr. and Mrs. Cut Meat, Double Wound, and John Y. Nelson, whose wife was pregnant. Despite their trust in Cody, many were terrified about "going behind the sunrise," which was exactly how a ship disappearing over the horizon appeared. Those who stayed behind in New York were unable to force themselves to leave dry land for a water venture they were convinced would lead to foreordained disaster.

There were more than 160 horses, including my two. We brought an assortment of North American animals: sixteen to eighteen buffalo, about ten elk, two deer, two bears, five Texas steers, ten mules, and four donkeys. To top it off, we had the Deadwood stage disassembled and nailed into a big box in the hold. All day long, lines of people and animals crowded the planks, squeezing together to make room for the loading of cart after cart of belongings and supplies.

At the dock, I had a teary moment bidding goodbye to Shea. He seemed a bit tentative himself.

—You don't know how you might change so far away, or who you might meet to change your mind.

—Don't be silly, Shea, Annie burst in. Abigail wouldn't leave you holding the bag with the Pinkertons.

I could sense both Shea and I were smiling, even as we avoided looking at each other. I pulled out my father's watch from my pocket.

—Here, I said to him. This was given to me by my father as a gift from my mother. It is all I have left of them, and I am giving it to you so you know I will come back.

As we waved goodbye to Shea in a crowd that floated away, growing evermore small and quiet, I slumped onto my steamer trunk.

—Aren't you excited about going home? Annie asked.

—I am leaving a dead father to return to a dead mother. Either direction, I have only sadness.

—Well, then, you need to create new memories.

I smiled gloomily.

—I am perfectly serious, Abigail. Your parents are dead, that is true, and a fact that is not going to change. Are you going to be miserable all your life over something you can do nothing about?

—I know you are trying to cheer me up, Annie, and I appreciate it. But thinking about England makes me see how unrealistic my plans have become. I do not want to be a stable-hand for the rest of my life. You know very well I am not good enough to earn my living from shooting.

—Why are you so worried about making a living when you have January's money?

—I am giving that back—to someone. I just don't know who yet.

—With time and practice you could make yourself a fine and credible professional shooter.

—Time may well be my downfall. I could go back to New York and wind up in jail for life.

—Shea will not allow that to happen.

—You know there is no way he can guarantee it.

She crouched down in front of me to claim my complete attention.

—I am telling you we will not allow that to happen. If there is one thing I have learned in my life, it is that you have to go into your future with the confidence it will be there for you and the determination to get there. We will make sure that right is done in the end. The only question is how, and now is too soon for the answer.

Bigger problems on our ship put my worries into perspective. The Indians were right about our trip being disaster bound. A violent storm smashed our rudder, leaving us tossing about without direction for forty-eight hours before the captain secured us back onto our route. It was a spooky sound to hear the death songs of seasick Indians rising up from the hold. During the worst of the storm, Annie spent ten hours wrapped in oilskin and strapped to the captain's deck. If he refused to leave the deck in the midst of trouble, she was going to be right there with him. Once she eventually returned below decks, I was in fine survival form myself, tending to seasick children and calming my skittish horses.

Sunny skies and a repaired rudder curtailed the death songs but brought new problems because Annie had to share deck space with Lillian Smith, whom she now described out loud to others as a hippopotamus. Sorely tempted to miss her target close to the shooter's head, Annie had to fight for her self-discipline. Everyone would know she was too accurate a shot to have so fortunate an accident. At the end of April 1887, the *State of Nebraska* finally wobbled into Albert Dock, and we began our wagon train to the twenty-three–acre grounds we would occupy near London.

Almost overnight, we built the kind of town that had so recently been raised on Staten Island and again in Manhattan. We opened to half a million Londoners who came to see the Yankeeries, as they called us. Major Burke had come ahead of us to secure advertising and set up interviews. Britons got to know us through the newspapers, which meant reporters came out every day to interview as many people as they could about what the show had to offer, each day becoming more and more focused on Annie. They were heady days. Twenty to thirty thousand excited fans streamed into our show every twenty-four hours.

Annie met William Gladstone, the former prime minister; Edward, Prince of Wales; the Grand Duke Michael of Russia; and ultimately Queen Victoria herself. Showered with flowers and gifts of silk and lace, photographs, and figurines, she outshone any attention ever paid to Lillian Smith, who was deliciously accused by James Carter of cheating. He charged that in the stunt where she claimed to have covered up the sights of her rifle with a card, she had cut away peepholes.

Tall tales about all the performers abounded, since we were the usual feeding ground for journalists. Whether these inaccuracies were fed to the press by the interviewees themselves or our press agent, or were simply made up by the writers, no one knew one way or another.

Some stories had Annie born in Kansas instead of Ohio, and many more told of her trapping wolves for Indians instead of shooting grouse for hotels. She foiled train robbers and shot bears. The wilder the stories, the more people loved them. She told some of the journalists that she agreed with her compatriot Mark Twain when he said,

"If you don't read the newspaper, you're uninformed. If you read the newspaper, you're misinformed." They thought the sentiment charming and seemed not the slightest bit insulted by the criticism.

The Indians in the show liked England well enough. They called Queen Victoria "Grandmother England," and Black Elk was heard to posit that perhaps if she had been his people's grandmother they all would have fared better. I invited Annie to visit my Cornwall relatives, who had recently moved to London. She was happy to go to find out what regular English folk were like outside of a rodeo show.

Annie had always thought the British were a quiet sort. When most of them were female and all in the same room, quiet was not an accurate description. There was much crying over Father, which also made Annie cry because it reminded her of her sick mother back home. My cousins were astounded to hear I was part of the Buffalo Bill Wild West Show, and grew positively raucous when I told them who Annie was. Around a dining room table laden with teacups and crumpets, I answered questions.

—Did you go for walkabouts in the wilderness of Canada? little Meagan wanted to know.

—The wilderness is not simply a forest, I told them. There is much brush underfoot, and you should really take a gun.

—A gun! they shrieked. What would you shoot?

I told them about moose and bear, mentioning the possibility of hunting rabbit.

—Will your show leave Indian artefacts at the Royal Museum? asked another.

—Of course not, I said. The Indians are employees, just like Annie and I are.

—Once your adventure is done, you will surely come back to teach at your old school.

—I do not want to teach anymore.

—What will you do? several called out together.

—I will continue to practise my shooting with Annie. Other than that, my future is a bit uncertain.

—But you will stay on in England now that you are back! cried my aunt.

—Actually, the one thing I know for sure is that I will be returning to New York.

—Whatever for? the chorus exhorted.

I glanced at Annie as she caught my eye.

—I made a promise to someone that I would come back.

At that the crowd became insistent. Why would one make such a promise? Was it the person or the promise that was important? They could demand to know, but I did not have to answer. Soon Annie thought it time to chip in her two cents' worth to shore me up.

—Why would anyone choose an old world when faced with the chance for a new one? she advanced pleasantly.

—That is just like you Americans, they laughed. All you think of is new, new, new!

—Well, Annie said, call me guilty as charged on that one.

She even added Mark Twain's observation that "an Englishman is a person who does things because they have been done before. An American is a person who does things because they haven't been done before."

As I looked around the table at my relatives, I could see how painfully out of place I had become. No longer part of any world that fit me, I was wedged between stable-hand and whatever awaited me once I faced the music with the Pinkertons.

A month into the show, I received Shea's first letter.

Dearest Abigail,

I am writing to keep you posted on my progress with the guns. As we discussed before you left, I made the arrangement to meet with Robert Pinkerton at the New

York office. He was suspicious about why I wanted to give back guns that would otherwise bring a high price for their alleged notoriety. He was unconvinced that I acted as an agent, and jaded about our concern that the deceased detective's next of kin be notified. I am encouraged, however, that he wanted to verify whether the mother-of-pearl gun did, in fact, belong to their detective. His interest indicates some commitment to pursuing the facts.

Next month I plan to travel to the Pinkerton head office in Chicago, where I have an interview scheduled with the other brother, William. Apparently the head office has the equipment and experts to verify whether this particular gun belongs to their detective. I assume that a positive identification will be the last barrier to notifying the relatives. In the meantime, I shall go to Stillwater to see if the Younger Brothers might be able to shed some light on January's gun. If there is no dispute about the owners of the guns, our issue narrows to what happened to the owners.

Despite the puzzle of why January thought of Annie and me as the proper inheritors of his last wishes, so far he was right in his conviction that they would be carried out according to plan. I am looking forward to seeing you again.

Shea

I wrote my response and showed it to Annie.

Dear Shea,

Our show proceeds exceedingly well, and Annie is the toast of the town. Despite all the excitement, though, my thoughts are constantly back in New York, worrying about you and all I am putting you through.

It is too much to ask for you to go to Chicago. Granted, it is understandable that the Pinkerton brothers are suspicious of my outlandish story. I can only hope their interest in the truth will allow us all to bring closure to this sorry circumstance. I console myself with the knowledge that you and Annie and I are all in this somewhat together.

I do appreciate your having taken this project on with such determination. Please reimburse your expenses from the money you hold in trust. January expressly told me to pay out all expenses. Of course, since it was stolen money, it was not his to direct, but the expenses are more than justified.

I await all news with bated breath.

Yours,
Abigail

Although there were other letters over the summer, they contained no reference to the case until September, when all of us received the same form letter that Wyatt had evidently sent to his friends and acquaintances.

Dear Friends,
As you may know, two guns have come into my possession, one owned by a Pinkerton detective who was fatally wounded when he attempted to shoot an outlaw named Shep January and in so doing shot at an innocent bystander. Mr. January died of cancer several weeks later. Mr. January is rumoured to have ridden with the Jesse James Gang and is believed by some to have been

involved in the Northfield Bank robbery of 1876, for which the Younger brothers are still serving sentences in Minnesota's Stillwater Prison. The Pinkerton Company has verified that the detective's gun, distinctive for its mother-of-pearl handle, belonged to their employee, who was supposed to be working in Minnesota but tracked January up as far as Manitoba and then into Ontario.

The Pinkerton brothers wish to dispute the accident as I have presented it, and instead want to call it a murder. Despite the goodwill of my client in turning over the guns of both the outlaw and detective, the Pinkertons claim they have new evidence that contributes to their case against me as a lying perpetrator. Since I am entirely innocent, there is something nefarious at work in this supposed evidence. Be that as it may, I write to you from a jail cell in Chicago on a charge of murder in the first degree.

In a rush to justice, my trial has been set down for November.

Yours truly,
Shea Wyatt

Shea had warned me to brace myself for sudden setbacks. He maintained that knowing the direction of an attack helped with its defence. Anguish gnawed as I pictured him confined. Here I was back in the place where my rash decision-making started. Thankfully, Father would never know how much worse the calamity of our grand adventure grew. I was prepared for something happening to me. I caused it all in the first place. Even behind bars, I would still have Shea to help me, but he was alone in that cell with no one. And for something I conscripted Annie to help push him into. She could not blame me as much as I did myself.

People were taught to be loyal to family members. I did not have any siblings, and Annie was too young to recall her biological brothers and sisters with any clarity. And yet, we both agreed that blood was not thicker than water. She and Shea would not feel any sense of duty toward the family spendthrift or sloth just because he was related. Loyalty to bloodlines corrupted Europe, as far as Annie was concerned, and flew in the face of what America stood for. She insisted that her rescue of Shea as a child was no act of altruism. She would never immolate herself for a higher purpose. Instead, in his vulnerability she saw the call to fight evil, the way she once fought it for herself. Evil needed to be fought whenever it was encountered.

Why was she unafraid as a child to confront the drunk grocer who beat Shea to a pulp? The grocer would do the same to her in the same condition if given half a chance. With a gun in her hand, she knew she could beat back the monster. Shea looked up to her as one he could count on to make his world safe, to stare down evil and make room for the good to thrive. She would never disappoint him. For him, for her, she would make sure that was the way the story ended. She quoted Mark Twain yet again, declaring, "The trouble is not in dying for a friend, but in finding a friend worth dying for." Shea was family, not mere kin. He was her good in the world. She could protect him and herself. If Annie could have shot William Pinkerton from across an ocean, she most certainly would have done so.

The day I received Shea's letter, I charged into Annie's tent.

—I am going to leave on the next ship, I told her.

—I understand, she said.

—This is worse than anything I expected.

—Then you have a limited imagination.

—There must be something we can do.

—There usually is.

—We will talk when you get back.

She hugged me.

Her stories instructed me that anyone who denied fair treatment to her or anyone she loved had chosen her as an enemy and could expect her to act. I suspected January somehow knew this as he plotted how to draw me into his plan. What could he have known about the possibility of this turn of events? It did not matter. No matter what he did or did not do, what he did or did not know, he had swept us all into the same whirlpool.

I docked on US soil in early November. My first stop was Shea. As I arranged my visit, I half expected to trigger some reaction, but no one singled out my name. Shea informed me he took the guns first to Robert Pinkerton at his New York office earlier in the summer. The head of a feudal army of industrial police, he looked more like a banker with a compulsive habit of pushing his round spectacles up the bridge of his nose against his forehead. The detective listened intently to Shea's report and noted that Shea's client was out of the country for now. He expressed some surprise when advised that I had signed an affidavit attesting to all I had done. He was even more surprised that I would expose myself on my return to be interviewed by any authorities deemed necessary. He counselled Shea to take the matter to Chicago, where his brother William could arrange for verification of the guns' ownership.

Soon after, Shea booked his passage on a westbound train to Minnesota's Stillwater Prison. Since the Younger brothers had no particular reason to answer his questions about January's gun, he considered how he might encourage their cooperation. He sent a letter to the warden ahead of time, outlining what he needed to accomplish and asking permission to show them the gun. He also addressed a letter to all three brothers, wherein he said only that he had a client who would like him to deliver a message to them about Shep January and request their assistance in identifying his gun. Whether they still felt some fraternity with their comrade, or simply craved some entertainment to interrupt what must have been long days, they agreed to see this stranger.

Seated along one side of a table in the visitors' room, the three benign middle-aged men in prison garb looked out of place. Shea brought the gun in a box, which he left with the guard, who brought it to the table for them.

—I don't know how well you and January knew each other, he said, or how well you knew each other's guns. I thought that seeing his gun might trigger some sort of recollection of a significant detail.

Cole Younger, the first to pick it up, turned it slowly as he inspected the barrel, bullet, chamber, and finally the handle.

—Lotta stories people come to tell turn out to be made up. Reckon you can't believe everything you hear. Had a man claim he bought my gray horse that I rode out of town after Northfield. I know my horse was chestnut and that it was killed right out from under me on the street. I never said a word to him. Another man said he saw all of us ride through his home town in Iowa on our way to Northfield, said he could see our guns in our belts. Fact is, we took the train and bought our horses in St. Peter.

—My client is not looking for money or fame. She wants to prove that the man she met was, in fact, Shep January so that she can attest to the fact that he died.

—How's he supposed to have died? Jim Younger asked.

—Cancer.

—Why she want to tell somebody that? Cole asked.

—He wanted it known. He said he wanted people back home to know he went out by natural causes. A Pinkerton was on him but never got him.

—What happened to the Pinkerton?

—My client happened to be standing between January and Pinkerton when the Pinkerton shot at January. My client shot back in self-defence.

The three men did not look at each other, but Shea had the sense they were passing a smile as surreptitiously as a spare ace in a poker game. Bob spoke for the first time.

—The Pinkerton was shot by a woman?

—She did not intend to kill him.

—You there?

—I did not meet her until she hired me for her defence.

—Imagine January got a laugh out of that one.

—I believe my client did mention a reaction very much like that. At that they all laughed out loud.

—What are you going to do with the gun, Jim asked. Sell it?

—It was Mr. January's property, so it should go to his next of kin, if he has any.

Cole turned the handle on its side and slid a sliver of wood off the heel. Burned into the flip side of the lid were the initials SJ.

—It's his gun. Glad to hear he went out on his own.

Because he thought January's gun would be the more difficult of the two to identify, Shea boarded the train for Chicago, pleased with his progress. He could bring this information to his meeting with William Pinkerton, nicknamed "The Eye" from the company's slogan *The Eye That Never Sleeps*. The only testimony about the actual shooting would be mine. Ultimately, my word had to be seen as sufficiently credible to carry the day.

As for the other gun, Shea conceded that going to Chicago to see William Pinkerton in May of 1887 was a bad choice. The Pinkerton brothers' father, Allan, had died the year before, bequeathing his company to two sons who were determined to prove themselves their father's equal. After the Pinkerton Company arranged for a firebomb to be thrown into Jesse James' mother's house, blowing off her arm, the name Pinkerton had fallen into disrepute, despite the self-congratulatory detective stories concocted by Pinkertons at the direction of the old man. The harder he tried to convince America that his ends justified his means, the more readers sided with the outlaw. Now the old man was gone, and a new staple of their business was the lucrative enterprise of divorce spying. This was the baggage in the Pinkerton office when Shea opened their door and walked in to meet William Pinkerton.

Perhaps William Pinkerton had not anticipated Chicago's Haymarket Square blowing up the day before, or, if the more paranoid are to be believed, maybe he did. To be fair, it was probably an unfounded rumour that it was a Pinkerton who threw the pipe bomb that started the riot. However, the eight men arrested for being nearby at the time it happened were not given the benefit of the doubt.

In any case, on the day of his appointment Shea arrived at a Pinkerton office frenzied with news of the bombing. A brusque receptionist herded him into the den of William Pinkerton, a big man over two hundred pounds with jet-black hair and eyes to match. He knew of Cody's show because he had operatives stationed there for the pickpockets that fed on distracted crowds. As Shea laid out January's and the Pinkerton's guns on his table, William Pinkerton decided that it was an insult to suggest that a young woman had come by herself all the way from north of Lake Superior to return these weapons. He contended that Shea's lie was meant to taunt him.

This is one reason why Shea insisted that history does make a difference. Had he come at another time, William Pinkerton might have been more rational, less rabid, as yet not besieged by strikers and rioters. Later in his life, William settled down to share drinks and do business with professional thieves. Maybe if Shea had come at that time, William would have been more the comfortable couch he was to become.

To this I countered that he never became more forgiving, just more corrupt. Opportunity ruled his actions, no matter the particular year. We must both grant our inability to know what any other circumstance would have brought.

Shea placed the guns carefully on the desk in front of Pinkerton.

"I'll be in touch," Pinkerton said without looking up.

Shea heard nothing about the case for the balance of the summer, until September, when two police officers showed up to bang on the door of his New York office.

"Mr. Shea Wyatt?" one asked.

"That is me," Shea answered. He went to his desk to retrieve my affidavit and support paperwork.

The police were not there for his affidavit. Pinkerton had done his homework. They had a warrant for his arrest for murder in the first degree. In short order he was charged and removed to a Chicago jail.

TEN

Chicago and Minnesota, September 1887 to May, 1888

TRIED

Despite Shea's admonishments against throwing myself to the wolves out of a misguided sense of protectiveness, I left him in his New York cell and headed straight for the train to Chicago. At first William Pinkerton's secretary refused me an audience, parroting that old argument that a trial should not be discussed until it came before the courts. The open sesame was my announcement that I had new information that Mr. Pinkerton would want to know.

His inner sanctum smelled of old cigar smoke and sweat, which Shea had not mentioned. Much thinking and sweating must have transpired between our visits, not to mention the smoking.

—I am sure you do not want to convict an innocent man, I began. Theoretically, it was the least risky opening. The Pinkertons were known for their generosity to repentant criminals as much as they were for their doggedness in executing revenge for Pinkerton murderers. However, I was quite sure my accusation that the Pinkertons were persecuting an innocent man did not sound much like repentance.

—You said there was something new, he growled.

—The one you want is me. I shot your detective. I did not intend to hit him. Believe me, I was more surprised than he was. But he did shoot at me from behind. Twice. What would you do if you were an innocent bystander and someone tried to shoot you in the back?

—Your Mr. Wyatt showed me your affidavit. You can take it to the judge and hope he believes you.

—Why would I lie? I had him bring the guns here to tell you what really happened. If you want the truth, we are on the same side.

—Look, he said, picking up his silver lighter from the desk and puffing his cigar to life, I have been in this business long enough to know that truth means different things to different people. I am more interested in putting the criminal I have behind bars.

—But Wyatt was hundreds of miles away!

—My truth is that nobody messes with a Pinkerton. Our trusting clients need to know that, the criminal world needs to know that, and you of the alleged lucky shot need to know that.

—But—

—If you were to read in the newspaper that a Pinkerton operative was killed by a young woman who randomly aimed to return his fire, and you wanted to hire one of the fourteen detective agencies in Chicago, what would your impression be of this one?

—I would think something had gone terribly wrong. I would think he made a stupid mistake, which he did.

—Does that sound like the kind of company you would hire?

—But what about the facts?

—You have your facts and we have ours.

—That does not change the truth.

His eyes burned bright with his own sense of power, despite the indulgence he pretended by smiling.

—That is for the judge and jury to assess.

—Mr. Pinkerton, what happened that day is not what you are making it out to be.

—See you in court.

Jurisdictional wrangling ensued about whether the trial should proceed north or south of the border, since all that could be definitively established was where the body was dumped rather than shot. It turned out the Pinkerton I shot was working out of Minnesota, so it was settled that Shea would be transferred there for his trial. On the day of the proceedings, the courthouse was full but not to overflow capacity as everyone had expected. Perhaps it was the biting November weather in Minnesota. Or maybe public outrage had already been spent on trials about dead Pinkertons. The Chicago anarchists from the Haymarket riot had all been convicted in June and were now ensconced in their appeals against what would turn out to be a mass hanging by the time it was done. The Pinkertons were probably disappointed that Shea's courthouse was not better attended for another round of example making.

A courtroom, I discovered, has its own distinctive sounds, especially when there is nothing you can do but look on and worry. An attorney was forever busy with speaking to court officials and organizing his paperwork. Shea was at the defence table, and Annie and I in the audience had nothing else to do but notice the sounds around us. Before the proceedings were called to order, conversation floated like gauze over the assembly, making the tones of the voices more important than the meanings of the words. Whether acquainted with the accused or the victim, associated with counsel for the prosecution or defence, or merely there to witness the carriage or miscarriage of justice, everyone's awareness was cued to the accused, and all knew why he was there. He sat at the table for the defence in what must have felt like surreal isolation.

Court conversation was not the festive gabble of an audience waiting to be surprised and amazed at a Bill Cody performance. No matter
how much chit-chat was devoted to what the audience members had
with their coffee earlier that morning, or who was sitting with whom
on the other side of the court, there was no mask for the sound of
lip-smacking anticipation.

Once the proceedings were heralded by the "all rise" for the judge's
entrance, the pageant began: directions to sit or stand, choreography of
counsel approaching and retreating from the bench. Throughout the
trial, the accused was the lightning rod for overwrought imaginations
picturing him, so tame and well dressed now, the way he must have
looked as a villain running free. Unless subjected to the rare instance
of giving testimony, an accused was immersed in the swell and ebb of
indoor and outdoor sounds: murmuring voices, shuffling feet, whinnying horses, and youngsters outside calling to each other in a game of
ball. All the while, I visualized my transparent self getting up, excusing
myself along the row of seats as though at a theatre, grabbing Shea,
and walking out the door.

On the first day of testimony, several witnesses attested to the
ownership of Pinkerton's gun. Exhibits of drawings in minute detail
were supported by the testimony of several fellow operatives. Since
identification was not a contested issue in the case, there was no need to
spend so much time on it, but the prosecutor doggedly built his image
as a close and careful researcher of facts. An expert on the Jesse James
Gang testified about January's gun, suggesting a number of the gang
members bought their guns from the same gun shop and apparently
favoured certain makes and models.

Although no one else had gone to ask the Youngers, it did not
matter, since the ownership of that gun was also not in contention.
What I could not figure out was how the prosecution would turn this
verification of everything they had so openly and willingly been told
into evidence against Shea.

Next came an officer of the North-West Mounted Police, all the way from Kenora, to testify about what happened after William Pinkerton contacted the police with a request to dig up his agent from the rocky terrain behind the village of Wabigoon. Testimony included a recitation of steps taken to locate the shallow grave according to information provided to them by the accused. Also confirmed was the grave of another man at the opposite end of a narrow shelf of ground, later identified as one Shep January. The Pinkerton carried no identification papers on his person, but had been identified visually by William Pinkerton.

The officer related results of his investigation among the villagers regarding any suspicious activity observed by them during the months of May through October 1885. Most often mentioned as the source of interviewee information was a man who offered himself as spokesperson for the villagers, and who all other interviewees agreed best knew the young woman who claimed to be the perpetrator of the shooting. Mr. Larsen swore an affidavit to the effect that Miss Abigail Peacock was a fine, upstanding teacher until her father died, at which point she took leave of her senses and disappeared. Until that time, she was known as a solid citizen to all the townsfolk and seen each day as a teacher in the local school.

Interviewees agreed that unidentified men coming and going from the area was a common occurrence, and all were adamant to note that although Miss Peacock was known to have purchased a rifle at Mr. Larsen's suggestion and was practising with it, she had not the temperament to shoot anyone, the strength to bury anyone, nor the constitution to keep anything like that secret from her fellow citizens. The autopsy verified that the Pinkerton agent had been shot in the chest by a bullet that matched the kind sold to Miss Peacock by Mr. Larsen, and that the agent seemed to have died instantly from that wound. Apart from character evidence about my temperament, nothing countered our version of the shooting.

Finally, a woman who identified herself as a midwife was summoned to the stand. Fiftyish as best I could tell, with a pleasant face and clearly frightened to be here, she avoided looking at Shea as the prosecutor began the inquiry.

—Did you, on or about July 1861, attend at a farmhouse in Drake County, Ohio, for the purpose of delivering a child?

—Yes, I did, she answered.

—And can you tell us in your own words what happened while you were there and who was in attendance with you?

—Well, sir, I came in answer to a call by the young lady's mother, who was known to my mother as a friend of a friend who lived in another part of the state. This was at the beginning of the war, and I was taking my chances travelling in the dark. I didn't care that it took a while to find the place because I was determined to help, especially since I knew the birth in progress had already run into complications.

—Who else was there?

—A young man, very distressed.

—Who was he?

—I was told he was the father-to-be but also a soldier on the Confederate side. For obvious reasons, he could not stay for long lest his presence send up an alarm in the district.

—Did you have a name for this Confederate soldier?

—Yes, sir, his name was Shep January. I heard the others call him that.

—And what happened with the birth?

—Despite every procedure I knew, I could not stem the internal bleeding for that poor creature. The baby boy lived, but the mother faded even as Mr. January desperately called out to her. I have never seen a man so distraught. He barely knew where he was when fellow soldiers strong-armed him from the room to a wagon they had waiting outside.

—What happened to the newborn from there?

—The little beggar was destined for the poor farm until a few hours later, when word came that the sheriff and his wife would come and get him. The sheriff's last name was Wyatt, and they named the boy Shea.

I hung in suspension with the rest of the courtroom as we all processed this information. The midwife was talking about January until the moment I grasped that she was talking about Shea.

For all those years that he saw himself as a sheriff's son, he actually was a sheriff's son. He sat at his father's table, ate his food, listened to his stories, absorbed his values, readied himself to defend whatever father taught son was right and true. When in his ninth year his father was killed by a drunken coward who had already killed his own wife, the father he grieved was one who had upheld the law as it had come to be understood in the Union territory of Ohio.

Like Annie's mother, Shea's mother also sold off all her belongings until eventual destitution forced her to indenture her three children if they were to be fed. When Annie came to his rescue at the grocer's, he was a sheriff's son fallen on hard times. He met Annie when he was ten, and five years later thought he was being delivered back to a normal family life when his mother remarried and they were all reunited. Within months of this second marriage she became pregnant and later died in childbirth, leaving the new husband with a baby and the immediate need for a new wife. Sixteen by then, Shea did not need to be told he was now an unwelcome guest to a stepfather he hardly knew. He never met the newborn half-brother baby. The circus provided an instant family, including an elephant handler who, out of the goodness of his heart, tutored the circus children.

Never in any of our wildest imaginations could we have suspected he was the son of an outlaw. How would he have interpreted his life had he known? Would he have seen his adoptive father's death as atonement for his bad blood? Maybe he would have been quicker to defend himself against that miserable grocer. He might have considered a wider range of options in saving his own skin, like cracking the grocer's head while he was asleep and taking off with the money in the hotel. The son of a sheriff would not think that way, but here he was, an accused murderer and the son of an outlaw.

For all we knew, the midwife could have been paid by William Pinkerton to make up what she said. If we could tell an honest face just by looking at it, we would have no need for the considerable expense of a criminal justice system. All the same, there was something about that midwife's face that convinced us she was to be believed.

I marched to the stand when Shea's defence counsel called on me to explain in detail how I had been teaching myself to shoot, how January had survived his fever, how the Pinkerton had surprised me with gunshots that prompted me to defend myself. The prosecution asked several questions about my father's deteriorating health, insinuating I likely made up fantasies to deal with my grief. He expressed his heartfelt condolences and asked if my relationship with Shea was in any way romantic. I flushed, and I could see some jury members smile.

Shea took the stand, already branded an outlaw and therefore expected to lie. His lawyer led him through the week he was alleged to have travelled by train to Wabigoon to commit the murder and back again. He was either working alone at home on articles about Annie, or at the office alone working on cases. With Annie on the road and none of his cases scheduled for court that week, there were no witnesses to testify for him. In cross-examination, the prosecutor doggedly pursued Shea's relationship to Shep January, making each denial sound suspicious. No one believed that a father would send his guns with a stranger—a young female teacher no less—alone over hundreds of miles that his son could more easily have travelled to help him.

Whatever personal integrity the jury sensed in Shea also worked against him. He seemed like a son who would remain loyal to his father. By the time the trial concluded, January looked like the criminal he was, I looked like I was shielding Shea, and Shea looked like he had protected a father with whom he had shared a longstanding secret relationship. They assumed Shea's commitment to his outlaw blood trumped the influence of the sheriff who raised him. January was in trouble with a Pinkerton chasing him, and Shea came to his aid willing to do whatever was necessary to protect him. It did not take long for the jury to return a verdict of guilty as charged.

Shea was to serve his time for the good people of the state of Minnesota in their Stillwater Prison. The Younger brothers expressed astonishment the day Shea showed up on their side of the bars. He could see they were model inmates, often delivering fresh laundry, inmate mail, tobacco, or the small library on a trolley to lend out books. They were housed in the cell across the corridor from his and often passed the time of day with him. He was inclined to categorize them as protective uncles, but they never let on whether they knew he was January's son.

I was the one doing most of the talking throughout those months. Having secured a room at the local hotel, I came to visit often, which Shea insisted was unnecessary. In the delay between the verdict and the appeal hearing, we had debates that were both heated and repetitive. For the first few weeks, I became incensed whenever he asked how he could know who he was without knowing where he came from, and who his ancestors were.

—So what if you are not who you thought you were? I demanded time and time again. How can we know exactly what we inherit from our ancestors? I am who I am, no matter who my father was. You deserve what your own actions warrant, not some ancestor's.

Doggedly, he insisted it made a difference to him, and peppered me with questions about January.

—Do not romanticize him, I retorted. He was a mean, twisted, miserable excuse for a human being.

—Somehow he kept track of me. All those years ago he gave me the money to become an attorney.

—He robbed and killed for that money, just as he did for the money he gave me to leave Wabigoon. You turned your money toward good.

—You still think of the law as good? he demanded.

—The law is not to blame for men's corruption of the facts. January did not care about laws at all, good or bad.

—He apparently cared about me.

—Maybe before the war he had promise. Believe me, there was nothing redeeming about him by the time he came to Wabigoon except that he could shoot a gun.

—Why do you suppose he wanted you to find me?

—So you could take care of his business. You should resent both of us for dragging you into this.

—He must have known people who knew me. How else would he know to find me through Annie?

—Where was he when you were with that grocer and needed some protection?

Shea accepted that as a good question. Why did January not come and rescue his boy then? It was understandable that January would keep his distance while the sheriff was alive. Once he died and the mother lost her children, what was worse, a child beaten as an indentured servant to a mean drunk, or a child brought up on the other side of the law by a father who knew how to protect him? Even if it was only for a few years, how could January have suffered watching Shea's mistreatment without interfering?

No one wanted to hear our petition that the jury had made a mistake. Riel was determined to prove the Government of Canada guilty of injustice so as to validate his rebellion. Shea, on the other hand, was convinced that his case was just as hopeless as Riel's argument.

—It is different, I insisted. The facts were not in dispute at Riel's trial.

—In my case the facts are fraudulent.

—Riel alleged the laws were wrong. He contended the Métis could not triumph in the white world of private property, and so he wanted to be compensated like an Indian.

—If he was right that the Métis could not compete in a white man's world, how would compensation change that once the money was gone?

—Riel knew what was wrong. He did not know how to fix it.

—Neither do we. And only the governor can grant a pardon.

One afternoon in early March, I decided I could wait no longer for Shea to make a decision about what to do. I drilled down to the question I had been circling for months.

—Do you have the moral right to rebel against those who render you an injustice?

Shea did not comprehend why this was important to me, even as the answer was evident to both of us.

—Abby, their use of fraud and coercion invalidates their own rights.

—Then you have a choice. Will you accept this injustice to support the law you think is right? Or, because of its unjust application, will you break the law to bring about justice?

—What do you mean?

—If your answer is to break the law for your own survival, then the question changes.

—To what?

—To whether or not you can pull it off. If your American fore-fathers could not have made their rebellion succeed, they would be sitting where you are right now. If Dumont had been able to fight the way he wanted, he might have saved Riel's neck. Perhaps he can be persuaded to help save you.

—And why would he do that?

—He does not like injustice any more than you do. He would

likely appreciate the chance to wage a war he could win. I could finance it with January's money and have some left over for a donation to his reparation fund.

—Abigail, you are suggesting a prison break, not a war. The government is never going to let a convicted murderer break out of jail and wander the streets living a normal life.

—If the governor could be convinced that a travesty of justice has occurred, perhaps he would be inclined to sign that pardon he is going to refuse at your appeal hearing. You could then come for an extended visit to Canada.

—Why would the governor do such a thing?

—Because it is right. I am convinced Dumont will agree. You are the one with the choice to make.

As we drew closer to the hearing date, these hypothetical debates escalated, the only difference being that I became endlessly preoccupied with the functioning of the prison. Until now, apart from the dream I recounted to him after having crossed the border into the US, I had not been concerned about the notorious Younger inmates. Now I wanted to know where their cells were situated. Did he see them each day? How much would they trust him?

Through his fog of memory during this period, he knew I was making a number of trips back to New York, but my comings and goings were confusing to him. We obviously decided that the Pinkerton Company was not to be trusted with returning stolen money. I was to consolidate January's funds in an account set up under my own name. Now that Shea was not earning an income, it would be needed for legal expenses until the appeal process was exhausted. I distinctly remember telling him I was bringing back Abe and Pinkerton so I could take care of them here.

What little hope he held out, he told me, lay in the public's mounting distrust of the Pinkerton Company. Last fall, a Pinkerton killed an innocent bystander during the Chicago stockyard strike. In January, a Pinkerton killed a boy during the Jersey coal wharves strike.

Shea hoped that perhaps the governor would have a twinge that I, too, claimed to be an innocent bystander, and that maybe my story did ring true.

I told him to continue dreaming if it made him feel better.

Shea had always thought of the justice system as foundational to civilization. Without it, we would suffer the rule of this world's bullies. Until now he had sat on the side of the bench where statistics were somewhat reassuring: juries were fallible but got it right most of the time. When it was your life they got wrong, what was the justice system then? A force for good that made a mistake, or the hostage-taker who cared nothing about truth?

The day came in May 1887 for the governor of Minnesota to hear Shea's appeal for a pardon. Both Pinkerton brothers had already arrived in town to oppose it. They were registered at the hotel in Stillwater where I was staying. After some investigating that morning, the desk clerk told me that they had an evening dinner reservation with the governor. An hour before we were to walk into the hearing, I told Shea what was planned.

—Are you out of your mind? he demanded.

—I am not really interested in your opinion. Decision time has come and gone.

—Abigail, you cannot just sweep into a prison and take out a prisoner because you think the jury and the governor made the wrong decision. What if everyone who felt the butt of injustice took the law into their own hands?

—And you do not think they have not or would not if they could?

—What has made you such a firebrand, Abby?

—You do not deserve this, and I am not going to have a life without you.

I reminded Shea that I came all the way from Wabigoon to New York to do right by the Pinkerton, and I came back from England to do right by him. I was going to break him out of jail for me. All I wanted from him was to draw me a map showing the way from the Younger brothers' cells to his.

What justification can be offered for a prison break? For one, he was innocent. Second, he had a stake in making his justice system worthy of respect. Third, if he stayed in prison, he would be torturing me, not sparing me. Last, he deserved his own justice. If he was not willing to fight for himself, why should anyone else help him? Shea hoped that was sufficient logic to justify what was to come.

DELIVERED

To Gabriel Dumont, Annie Oakley was an entirely different animal from the English and the Americans. She was a sharp-shooter. That she was a woman mattered less than the fact that he and she shared territory as fellow warriors. She had an enviable collection of six-shooters, a Colt, a Smith & Wesson, and a revolver with pearl grips. The night he spoke in her tent, she presented him with a gift, her own 1883 Parker Brothers shotgun. When she presented it to him, she declared it was to show they were family. Sitting Bull adopted her the year before as his daughter, and she now wanted to adopt Dumont as her brother who matched her in shooting. Because this shotgun was her own, it would remind him of their bond. Only because Annie Oakley was the best sharpshooter he ever witnessed did he honour her request to talk to the English girl. I was feeding the horses in another barn when Annie signalled that he would speak with me.

Just because he accepted Annie as a kind of family did not mean he would extend the same trust to the Canadian woman. I expected the experience of war to cause distrust. He was no doubt rightfully paranoid about not having amnesty from Macdonald. There could be bounty hunters, and his people told him I could shoot. She cautioned me not to stare at him because it made him edgy, like someone was trying to hide something.

I was lucky to find Dumont in a mood to talk about his story. He said his heart still hurt when he thought of the defeat at Batoche, and later what happened to his leader and friend, Louis Riel. For so long he thought back over what they did. He replayed it all in his mind to figure out how it could have been different. He did not like the Bill Cody Wild West Show so much, playing Indian for white crowds.

—I understand the importance of action. To make a decision even in the middle of chaos is not difficult for me.

We had not talked long before one of his men interrupted us with the news that a man had come to talk to him. I walked with Dumont to the stable doors, analyzing how strangers would know Dumont was here. Then I remembered Cody had a picture of him on the poster for the show. Dumont claimed that most of the time his eyes could see through a man and tell him if the stranger meant trouble. He was quick to clarify that he did not mean all the time because any man can be ambushed. Some are especially good at it, good actors, good liars, patient warriors. We both looked at this man standing at the stable door with the afternoon light shining behind him, where another man stood. Neither one had a gun.

—I am Gabriel Dumont, he told them both in French. Who wants to see me?

One man turned and spoke English to the other. The other looked at Dumont as he spoke English.

—He says his name is Howard, one man interpreted for the other.

—What does he want?

Dumont walked out the door into the sun, and it dawned on me bit by bit that he did so in order for his men to get a better angle, take their places inside doorways and behind open shutters to train their rifles on whoever might cause him harm. He said he did not fear violence because he knew how to return a fight. As a warrior, he knew he had to watch his back for tricks and traps. He said he knew this because his enemies should watch their backs from him.

—I do not know you. You look young to me.

—I was at Batoche, Howard said.

—Where are you from?

—Montana. I know people who knew Riel.

A surprise attack can happen against the mind as well as the body. He was not expecting the name Riel to be spoken by this man, and it hit him like a blow.

I could hear the horses snorting in their stalls. In a few hours, they would again race around the stadium in a mighty war of shrieks, stampedes, and bursting gunfire, before returning to sleep in the dark until morning. Louis Riel must have seemed very far from this place. The man looked like he had forgotten what he wanted, and Dumont was getting restive from the staring.

—You are American? Dumont asked.

—Yes, but I fought against you at Batoche. I was the gunner who fired the Gatling gun in front of the church. But that is in the past, and you won't hold it against me. In any case, I never shot at you. I wanted to test my gun in the field, so I shot in the air to frighten you.

When he finished, Dumont laughed.

—Oh no, I won't hold it against you, because you were hired to do that. But I did try to shoot you and put a bullet into your head. As for firing over us to frighten us, you are lying there. I know you did not shoot above me because the earth was flying into my eyes and all around me, and the small branches were being cut.

At this, Howard laughed too. He was on the same field of battle, and so could understand its importance even if they were on opposite sides. They were no longer enemies.

—What do you want from me? Dumont asked.

—All of us, the men who all fought together, have been trying to figure something out ever since. We want to know why you let him make you lose.

Dumont turned to me, inquiring if here was some English expression he did not understand.

—Make me lose?

—We knew you told your men to harass us all night every night to keep us awake and tire us out. You did it a few times, and you were right that we would have been at each others' throats if we had been sleep deprived and terrified for long. They say you wanted to blow up the CPR tracks. Is that true?

—You with Macdonald?

—No, no, I am not in the army. I went to Batoche to try out my gun. I keep thinking about what happened, and want to make some sense of it.

—I wanted to blow up the railroad.

—You would have been right. It would have scrambled the soldiers. You wanted to ambush the supply lines. If you had done it, we might have turned back. If you were winning, the Indians might have joined you. If you looked like you would take too many with you, Macdonald would have negotiated with you. Why did you let Riel make you lose?

Dumont had to look up and away so as not to grab Howard by the throat, and Howard could see that Dumont fought to control himself. I gave Howard this. He was not going to run away from Dumont until he got his answer.

—He had the vision.

—He was crazy.

—We asked him to come, and he saw the vision. I would not argue with a vision.

—Maybe he had a vision, but you let him decide your military strategy.

—God told him what He wanted. I can see you are not ruled by God, and this is now my struggle. The priests betrayed us at Batoche. I saw them go out to Middleton to tell them we had little ammunition or food, that a siege for any length of time would defeat us. I could not fight Louis, God, the priests, and Middleton's army all on the same day. Because of what the priests did, I lost my faith. Is it a loss of faith in the priests or in God himself? This is my question. I will never enter a church again. I have yet to decide if I will ever pray again.

—I didn't think they'd hang him, Howard said.

—We did not think it, but he knew it.

Riel had been quite vocal about his conviction that he was going to die. He wanted to die for God.

—The old way was to bow before God through the priests. Louis said God spoke directly to him, but I am coming to doubt that God speaks to anyone or through anyone. The old way was the buffalo. If God is speaking at all, it is in the disappearance of the buffalo. A man can be deluded about voices in his mind. Priests can lie about what God wants. There is no arguing with the fact that the buffalo are gone. I do not know why it happened, whether white people are to blame, whether God wanted Métis and Indian people to learn a new way, whether there is some other message in the disappearance, or whether there is no message at all.

—The world has changed before, Dumont continued. We all talk about the world left behind. There is a new way that is necessary for us to survive in this old land that has been flooded with the new. I begin to think about what our ways might be. No one talks about the world at our feet.

I turned to look directly into his eyes, whether he liked it or not.

—On this you and the English girl agree, I said.

It was the first time I ever saw this serious man smile.

The three of us sat down together against the wall in the sunshine while Dumont recounted his story of the Métis victory at Duck Lake, before Howard got there with his gun. Howard asked enough questions to inspire Dumont to go on to the story of Batoche. He told of how they dug their holes deep and dragged branches over them to hide. He laughed as he divulged to Howard that they watched soldiers standing above them scratching their heads about where the enemy had gone before Dumont's men opened up with shots of their last bullets that had to hit their marks. Dumont never knew the English could run so fast. Howard said for three days the soldiers talked about breaking the Métis line of defence by making them unload all the ammunition that was left.

Louis would not let Dumont lure the soldiers forward and attack from behind to seize their weapons and ammunition. He told Riel they should, but Riel said God did not want it. Their only luck was the carelessness of Middleton's volunteers. Some English left behind piles of cartridges after a day of fighting when they went back to their camp for the night. Dumont also found magazines from the Gatling gun that were an exact fit for their twelve-shot hunting carbines and kept the rebels going longer.

Dumont told Howard some of those bullets they found were the kind that exploded, the illegal ones because they blasted the flesh in all directions. The English themselves called these bullets a crime against humanity by civilized nations. He laughed when he told Howard this, and it was clear to me that his laughter was a form of condemnation.

A Frenchman named Paul Chelet, Dumont reported, counted the guns they had when they lost to the English at Batoche.

—We had seventy left. Chelet went to the English camp and asked an English officer how many men he thought the machine gun killed. The officer did not guess, maybe because he thought there would be trouble if he looked happy about dead Métis. Chelet told him he had counted, and the officer admitted he would like to know. "One," Chelet said. "And it was my horse."

Howard did not like to hear that. He had travelled hundreds of miles to show off his new invention that had contributed only a horse to Middleton's cause. Dumont clearly wanted to mock Macdonald for sending Middleton with thousands of soldiers and horses on trains to face a few hundred warriors who had sent him petition after petition.

After the reminiscing, Howard shook his hand and left, and I could sense guns being withdrawn as Dumont's men fell back to meet him at the Indian camp for dinner. He was tired from talking about all that, he told me. He came here to get American help for the Métis in repairing what Middleton had destroyed. They all longed to sit on their own front porches again.

Next day, I found him again and asked if we could finish our conversation. He told me he did not really like talking to the English. Annie told me there was trouble over in England with the Indians and some Métis he knew. Dumont could not go to England because his amnesty had not yet come through. Some Métis missed the boat over there and had to stay for a while for another one. Michel Dumas, who fought beside Dumont at Batoche, was always drunk so Cody threw him out on the street in Paris. Dumont said he knew this because Dumas went to the Canadian Consulate and said he was Gabriel Dumont. They brought him back to Canada as Dumont, maybe thinking he was more of a catch than he was. Jules Marion was the only one of Dumont's people he knew who finished his contract. Dumont thought that maybe, because I was the English girl, I knew about the troubles in England and France and was sent as a decoy by Macdonald.

I told him no, that I knew nothing about Macdonald. I was Annie Oakley's friend, and she wanted Dumont to talk to me.

—Your people think I am an outlaw. I do not think of myself that way. I respect authority so long as the authority deserves my respect. Americans want to know how an outlaw thinks, and so they ask about the moment I knew I had lost, when Middleton's forces stormed through Batoche. They ask those questions because they have never been warriors. What made me think of cutting the Northcote's steam stacks with the ferry cable? Why did the soldiers on board refuse to get off and rush back to the fight? The Americans think there is a secret and want the inside story. How could so few warriors hold off an army?

—My father died a year before your Madeline died of the same disease. Annie told me we have a bond of mutual pain and the common enemy of a disease.

—She told me the English girl has a proposal for me.

The night of his speech in Annie Oakley's tent, he learned I had come down from Canada to shovel out stalls for the Cody show. But that night I wore the kind of dress that made him think I was sent to talk to him about the amnesty. He knew about the amnesty already but did not trust it, and he did not trust me in that dress.

—They are a sneaky bunch, those English. On one side of their mouth they invite me to come home, and then they put a $5,000 bounty on my head. I am a leader of people. I have kept laws and given out punishment for breaking them. I wanted to make Americans interested in why we had a rebellion. I trade my story for donations to help my men. It is a trade, like guns for buffalo hide.

When Cody hired him, all he had to do was ride his horse around the arena. He did not care what the announcer shouted out as a story about him. The other Indians said the story was about him leading the force of the northern revolution against the English. Like the French in Québec, Americans also like hearing stories about fighting the English. Now that there was talk of an amnesty, he was no longer a ferocious rebel. Now he was a son to be forgiven, and so their interest seeped away, he said, like water from a summer creek. Even when the amnesty was announced and Cody said he could rip up his contract with the show, he did not trust Macdonald and would not go just yet. But he wanted to go because he was getting pretty sick of glass balls. The Indians laughed whenever he said that.

No longer in my suspicious dress, my boots and pants and hide jacket seemed to make him more comfortable. I did not come to tell him about the amnesty. I came to make an offer of a new story. It could never be the story he wanted, but it was pretty good just the same.

I told him that the American, Wyatt, who Annie Oakley called brother, was in jail for a killing he did not commit. I called myself the English girl, just to show I was not trying to trick him into thinking I was anyone but who I was. I told him the long and complicated story that made sense to him because he could see these Pinkerton men wanted something to be the case whether or not it was true. He had met men like that. He said he could also tell by my steady eye that I was telling the truth. I killed the Pinkerton because he shot at me. There was nothing wrong with that. The other man who died later wanted to be the one to kill the Pinkerton, but did not have the chance. I had the right to defend myself, but the Pinkertons wanted a murder by Annie Oakley's brother. He had the guns and was the son of the outlaw.

He said he could see Annie Oakley killing a man. He was surprised that the English girl who wore that dress had it in her.

Once the American cavalry let Dumont go free at Fort Assiniboine as a political refugee, he went to Spring Creek and raised money, arms, and warriors willing to hide Riel over the 450 miles from Regina to Lewiston, Montana. Just like the freedom train for slaves, he had an underground railway for Louis. Every ten to twenty miles he had food, horses, and men to provide an escort for the next stage of the trip. The underground railway went from south to north; Louis Riel would make that journey in reverse. He had planned an escape from jail for Riel, but Riel did not want it.

He told me of another time when Louis Riel's father was a young man. The Hudson's Bay Company would not let the Métis warriors trade with the Americans, who paid almost double for everything they trapped and traded to the Company. Carts went north and south through Pembina anyway because the Americans paid more. When the Company tried to stop them, they became more inventive in smuggling anything from pelts to letters, since the Company began to censor the mail too. British soldiers were brought over to stop the trading with Americans. While the warriors could not fight an army, they could lay low like buffalo to watch and wait for the right time to spring to their feet. After two years, the English soldiers went back to where they came from and gave the Métis the chance to fight it out with the Company that would take whatever it wanted right out of their mouths.

Their opportunity came when Guillaume Sayer and three other trappers were tried and convicted for trading their furs against the rules of the company. Five hundred Métis warriors organized by Riel's father surrounded the courthouse to proclaim that they would be taking Sayer and his men home to freedom, no matter what the court said. On that day, the court figured out a way to do the right thing. The Company could no longer be a tyrant, and the Métis learned that justice could be gained by an outside power if it was strong enough.

—The laws must serve more than just the few who make them, I said.

—I was leader of my hunt, the one who understood our Métis laws and determined who would be punished and who would go free.

—I cannot comment on how well you did that, I said, because I did not see for myself the decisions you made. But I can tell you that in my mind a culture rises or falls on its ability to treat people as they deserve to be treated. That includes punishment as well as exoneration. I do not care who makes the laws so long as they are just and are administered properly.

We nodded our acknowledgment that things are not right just

because they are old or just because they are new. They are right because they are right.

—This time you will not have to fight the Canadian army, I said. You will need to fight only the sheriff's posse. Maybe you were right or maybe you were wrong when you took up arms in Saskatchewan. I can say only what I know to be true, and I know that Wyatt did not shoot the Pinkerton.

His warriors in Saskatchewan sprang into action when that lying Lawrence Clarke told them five hundred police were coming for Louis and him before Duck Lake. This is what started the rebellion. The truth he found out later was that there were no more than eighty, but he believed this was their only chance to act. If he had known the truth, he would not have taken up arms. This was a fact he had to face.

—I am governed by no God, I said. And I will see no visions. As the general in charge of the men we hire, you answer only to yourself for your actions in accomplishing our purpose. Just like in a buffalo hunt.

He saw that I wanted the good to win out, and he was part of the good. Just as surely as he had wanted Riel out of jail, I wanted Wyatt out of jail. The difference was that Louis was surrounded by an army that expected him to try, while Wyatt's jailers had no idea what was in store.

—You can blow up whatever you deem necessary, I said, and recruit from the places where you have been visiting since you made your escape from Batoche. Build a private army, as many as you need. Break him out of Stillwater Prison in Minnesota and bring him to Canada. The United States has been your refuge. Canada will be his.

He heard me out, and I could tell the thought of becoming a military leader again tempted him, especially because his hands would not be tied this time. He must have craved witnessing the happiness on the faces of his men when he returned them to their farms with the money I pledged to donate after the prison break. But the temptation fell short when he considered that my plan offered only false hope.

He did not think this could be his story. It was about a white man who suffered the deceit of his own people. Wyatt's problem was no business of Dumont's. This one man's freedom did not change anything for the Métis. In the end, it made no difference to them whether a particular innocent white man went to jail. Dumont's people were overrun by strangers who interfered with his people's ways. He was made a leader to solve their problems. A prison break put him in danger of going to jail himself. He was a felon in his old country and an unwelcome guest in his new one. For him to gamble on getting wounded again, or killed, there would have to be a very good reason.

Dumont told Annie he would not help the English girl. His supreme responsibility to his people was to make sure they were not placed at risk on a whim. I was disappointed but respected his decision. He thought a weight would come off his shoulders, but he said that he continued to walk heavily because of thoughts about what might have been. One evening a week later, we performed the Deadwood Stage scene one more time, with him riding Abe for the entertainment of those who care nothing of the Métis. Afterwards, when he joined the Indians around a fire as he usually did, he asked himself if he was content to play-act further.

He started thinking that his people should know that things might have turned out differently. They did not lose because they were Métis. Other decisions could have produced other results. He began to picture himself riding back to his farm in Batoche to meet his old warriors. He could tell them something about themselves that Macdonald and Middleton did not know. He could give his warriors something to make them smile.

He struggled with a question: would the English girl's battle be a victory for his vanity or a victory for his warriors? He began to think my plan could be a victory for everyone. Wrong affected everyone.

Righting it, no matter the target, was righting it for all who looked on. Something was not true just because a certain person said it. Injustice was not wrong because of who received it. If we all stood by while injustice happened in front of us, we deserved no different ourselves. They tried to right a wrong in Batoche but could not. They had the chance of a victory here. I was mucking out a stall when his figure filled up the barn doorway. He came to tell me he had changed his mind.

—When the Europeans came and did not understand this new world, we taught it to them. When Indians wanted to trade with the newcomers, we taught them too. That those men no longer need us is no discouragement to us. We will think for ourselves as to what and who we value and judge. Even as we lose our way of life in the wilderness, we will learn about our new world and how to survive in it. If we see something is not right, we will fight it. This is why I decided to speak to my fellow Métis in the north of Minnesota, Montana, and the Dakotas—so they would know why we would break the rules of the American court and the Stillwater Prison.

Once more, Dumont organized his soldiers according to a buffalo hunt, with each captain knowing what to do from the moment of the first explosion. For this new mission, he ordered rifles, pistols, and dynamite. Eighty-five Métis signed up for the expedition before he had even finished explaining the reason.

There was no priest now, no crucifix held up to bless them, no spiritual guide. In one way he was sad not to have one along. There was much solace to be enjoyed from the certain knowledge of spiritual approval. In another way, though, it was not something given one day and taken away the next by priests who sympathized until they were out telling your enemies of your war strategies. Without the burden of the priests and their spiritual games, he was free to use his wits.

The first time I sought out Dumont was after Wyatt's guilty verdict in the court. I predicted the appeal would be rejected in the spring. On the day the governor did this, we should be ready to move. Annie and I both wanted to be deployed as warriors. If we failed, we would all fail together.

The day came in May, a day that reminded Dumont of the May in Batoche two years before, when he had to face the results of decisions made by Louis and God. When the battle started, the best he could get for Louis was a noble defeat. On this new day in May 1887, he woke up before dawn to greet the sun on his feet like a man with the chance to flourish. He made the promise of a commander: he would brook no interference.

If Louis had been with us, he would have had us stop every five minutes to say the rosary. As much as Dumont's heart was still broken, without Riel we could all work as one hunter stalking his prey. He had walked the grounds of Stillwater Prison in preparation, pacing off how far the prison was from the river, where would be a good landing spot for our canoe, how far to the warden's house, how long a posse would take to get to the prison. Those days he wandered and thought about these plans, he grew into the happiest man alive.

We began our war at the front of the prison at midnight, when the guards passed each other in the front office at their change of shift, some going home and others coming to work. When fifty of Dumont's men stampeded down the road out front to whoop and yell like Indians, they stirred the fears of all inside, inmates and guards, but were careful not to blow any bars. No one expected a day when attackers from the outside might try to get in. Warriors wailed around the building, rattling everyone inside with the memory of Colonel Custer. Dumont's men laughed as they watched the confusion and waited for the sheriff to get out of bed and rustle up his posse.

Once the skies had lit up like fireworks after a Cody show, Dumont and a few of his men answered the signal by pulling their canoe up onto the riverbank behind the prison. Even in the shadows he could see grins on faces all around him. The roar of dynamite sounded like God speaking. But it was not God at all.

Louis would have told him not to blow the iron door off the back of the stone wall because God did not want it. Louis always expected negotiation and did not like dynamite. Dumont knew that people negotiate only when you are stronger than they expect. If they are afraid of you, they become reasonable. If they are not, they ignore you, lock you up, or kill you.

With the door to the river open, they had fifteen minutes. The guards at the front were too busy with explosions to discover the breach at the back. Dumont and his men stole through dark corridors while ghosts still in their underwear began to call out to the strangers in their midst. From my maps he knew his way straight to the Younger cells, where three older men leaned on their cell bars, gaping at the explosives. Dumont told them not to worry. They would be back safe and sound in a few days. They were just going for a little ride.

Seconds later, they reached Wyatt, already dressed and waiting in his cell. Once his door tore open, they heard in the distance the signal that the posse had arrived and that Dumont's warriors were leading them north. It would be only a few minutes before guards appeared for a cell check. They hurried the hostages out past prisoners calling after them to open their doors and let them come too. They vanished into the night in the canoe. Dumont could see his men's torches on land in the distance, moving beacons that would continue for many miles to the meeting place.

He was not afraid to be caught. There is not one mind for the one who follows the law and another for the one who breaks the law. There is only the decision. If we fight for what is good, the outcome does not matter. Whether he wound up in prison or on his porch in Batoche, he knew he would smile each time he thought back to that night. His eyes looked with pleasure on his cargo of Younger brothers and Wyatt, with twelve of his men paddling in silent concentration as they skimmed along a silver path over dark water toward the moon. He once wished he could be off this earth and up there on that moon.

This day, he wanted to be exactly where he was, and doing exactly what he was doing. That moment in the canoe, when he was speeding toward the moon and thinking about all his warriors, would live on for him as one of perfect peace.

At midnight, when the prison exploded into chaos, we opened up a new front at the hotel where the governor and the Pinkerton brothers would by now be long finished their steaks and port. Dumont warned Annie Oakley that she would be known, and me, the English girl, that I might spend the rest of my life in prison. That worry made no difference. I could not seem to convince anyone to put me in prison.

The governor was awakened by Annie Oakley's voice in his room.

—Good evening, Governor. I'd be much obliged if you'd get yourself dressed and come with me.

His outrage lasted only so long as it took him to notice he was staring down the barrel of her gun. If he considered calling out to bring help from the Pinkerton brothers, he probably would have thought again about winning a contest of speed against Annie Oakley.

Next door, the Pinkerton brothers were listening to me.

—Good evening, gentlemen. You might think it is time to sleep right now, but you are actually getting up and dressed. Your truth might be that you are contemplating calling for help because justice is being compromised. My truth is that you are going to silently haul your miserable souls down onto horses that you will ride through the night. Would you like to bet on whose truth wins this time?

Three of Dumont's warriors stood as backup, and twelve waited downstairs with horses. We fell into a long line over miles of territory well known to Indians and Métis of the Red River basin, up beyond Duluth to French River. The men were used to the long treks of a buffalo hunt, their carts and horses stretching in a line for days. Dumont's plan was for us to ride until the sun came up and down and up again on our parade north.

The sun was already high when Dumont and his men exchanged their canoes for horses.

—We will ride the rest of the way, he told Wyatt.

—Them too? Wyatt asked, looking at the three Younger brothers.

—We will take them with us. Annie Oakley and the English girl will bring the governor and Pinkertons soon. The posse will follow last.

—No matter what happens tonight, Wyatt said, I want to thank you for what you have done. Abigail, Annie, and I all regard you as a hero.

—Much can still go wrong.

—You have taken action for me when you didn't need to, and I would have understood if you had decided against it.

—It is not only for you that we take action, Dumont said. We have to live with what your ancestors brought, but we are part of what we will all become.

Annie and I rode with the governor and the Pinkerton brothers, flanked by another twenty of Dumont's men to ensure no escape. She talked without stop for all the time we rode. One of Dumont's men told me later that it was a punishment for all the men, white and Métis. They said among themselves in Cree that prison walls would be a relief from all the talk. With Annie, a discussion is really a listen-to-her-speak.

In the distance we could see plumes of smoke Dumont's men had lit as guides for the posse trailing them along the route to Duluth. At French River, our two groups met up. Even Annie fell silent as we changed horses and men before striking north again through Chippewa country and the new railroad past Ely. They were on course for the Canadian border. No one could tell exactly where it was, since the hills and lakes showed no indications of a border, no line that made a difference to the land or the people who wandered through there. At the meeting place, no one would know which side of the border we were on.

The day Dumont rode from Batoche to Montana, President Cleveland said he was not to be held by the cavalry because he was a political prisoner. In the space of one step over a border, he became a different man. One hanged and one went free.

He planned his ambush for the section of road that curved through a pass between two steep hills. A man galloping on a horse down this stretch had no way of knowing what waited around the bend until he was through the pass and already facing his fate. Early in the chase, his men rode like the wind until they pulled eight hours ahead of the posse. After a night and day of riding, they slowly reduced the distance between them to two hours, making the predators think they were gaining and soon would be in position for the kill.

Wyatt, Annie, Dumont, and I lined up our horses across the road just beyond the point marked for the attack. The governor and two Pinkerton brothers sat behind us, with eight of Dumont's horsemen in rows behind them. As I sat and listened to birds squabble over scraps left from our camp, my mind focused on another camp less than two hours down the road, where Dumont's men would be mounting up for their last charge. They would ride from the east chased by a rising sun. As they advanced, the sun would burn off early morning fog to reveal a day different from all others.

The interpreter called out Dumont's orders as he gave them, so that all assembled understood what was about to happen without question. If the governor or Pinkertons attempted escape, they would be shot. He wanted the Younger brothers hidden in the bush out of the way. The rest of his men were to blend into the trees until needed. All eyes stared forward so intently that only the continued silence made us mistrust images of horses and men we saw moving in the mist. For those not used to facing death, that silence was torture.

The warriors had trained themselves to wait absolutely still, like an oak tree, strong no matter what force was brought to bear against them. Horses shifted their weight, shook their manes, and snorted when they stood too long. Men who acted like horses were the ones least sure of why they fought. With darting eyes and shaky hands, they were the first to run off. In every war there came a time—maybe just before a battle, maybe in the middle, for sure at the end—when all the shouts and blasts fell to a lull. The tornado that just ripped up the earth twisted away on a new course that left one tree torn up by its roots and the flower beside it completely untouched. No one knew where the fight would go next.

The governor's horse was especially restless.

—Are you going to shoot them in cold blood? the governor asked quietly.

Dumont's interpreter whispered English words to him as they were spoken nearby. Dumont told me it was not so hard to keep up with the English. Sometimes he already knew what had been said. People talked for a long time without saying much. He did not need his interpreter's words to read what the governor asked. Fear was its own language.

I could have answered him, since it was my war. Instead, I remained as still and quiet as a stone. My stare bored through the back of my horse's head.

—First our men will come, Dumont said. They will line up on both sides of the road to wait. Shooting will start as soon as your men ride around that bend. We will give them no warning.

Wyatt looked ahead of him, up to the sky, then over to me.

—We never said anything about slaughter.

His voice rang out clear and accusing.

I could feel Dumont's eyes on my hunched figure in the saddle, probably reminding him of Louis just before he related what God did not want him to do. He would avow an ability to see past the battle to the future. One day, it was a landscape of twisted metal, a destroyed railway track, all that work of hundreds of men decimated. Another, it was a vision of bodies in grotesque positions at the moment their spirits escaped. When he could not read Louis's face, he was usually sliding away from certainty. He was hearing God's displeasure and forgetting all Dumont told him about war, that if you declared it, you had already concluded that justice would not be volunteered by your enemy.

Dumont said he learned that wars were not won through worry over consequences. Victories were powered by conviction. His interpreter murmured in his ear Wyatt's argument for a compromise. Maybe they could negotiate a reduced sentence, maybe ten years. They had to work with what was possible. Killing an entire posse for the sake of one man was not justice.

The ground began to hum under us with the faint rumblings of hooves. When our lead rider thundered into view, his rifle held high, Dumont shot his finger into the air to motion a wide circle. Immediately he pulled the charge back on itself and split the men into twenty-five along each side of the road. We could hear them panting from the hard ride as we all watched for their pursuers.

The governor shifted in his saddle to turn around and face the Pinkerton men.

—These people here strike me as righteous, not guilty.

Dumont called out to his men that when he raised his arm, they would aim their rifles but no one would shoot until he brought his arm down. If anyone had itchy fingers and pulled a trigger before his signal, Dumont would personally shoot him dead. His interpreter's words transformed from Cree to French to English. From the nearby hills, his echo was the voice of a ghost reminding them the price to be paid for disobedience.

Annie pulled two rifles out from her side pouch to place on her lap, and cradled a third in the crook of her arm.

—I have never killed a man, General, she announced, but when you say the word, I'll get the first twenty.

The day they fought the English at Duck Lake, Louis left all decisions to Dumont. They cut telephone lines, took prisoners, seized supplies, set up their headquarters. When the English made a barricade of their sleighs in the snow, Dumont ambushed them. Even a bullet slicing a trough along the top of his head could not stop them. Outnumbered almost two to one, his brother dead in the snow, they prevailed.

Soon the sound of stampeding horses and excited men's voices raced down the road ahead to within earshot of our forces in the pass. Wyatt had stopped talking, but his stare remained fixed on me.

Dumont's attention was also trained on my face. He raised his arm. It hung there only a few seconds before I heard a cry.

—Don't!

Naked fear in the governor's voice.

—I will give you your pardon. Stand your men down!

Wyatt turned to him, more surprised than any of us.

—If this is a trick, Governor, we will shoot you, he said.

—I am not a stupid man, Mr. Wyatt. I can see you are in earnest. Give me the chance to stop this.

Dumont's arm remained in the air as he watched for me to drop my eyes, the way Louis used to do, or to shake my head. Slowly I raised my face, so slowly he could not have understood what I was doing until I pinned him with my eyes. My face was resolute, my nod undeniable.

Freed to do what he thought best, he signalled for his men to step back off the road and leave the governor to face his posse alone. Dumont scooped up the horses' reins and led them a few steps into the bush.

Horses detonated around the bend. One rifle report went off— someone breaching orders, whether one of his men or one of the sheriff's, I did not know. The governor flattened himself down against his horse's neck for protection against a stray bullet or even a collision with one of the posse riders who now swarmed him, some overshooting the unexpected obstacle in the road, unable to rein their horses to a sudden stop. After a few words from the governor, the sheriff looked around to notice for the first time a forest stocked with Métis warriors, rifles cocked to their shoulders. I could hear the shock in the voices. Some pointed out Annie Oakley.

This was how Dumont wanted his war with Macdonald to end. While the man in Ottawa was thinking about his last spike in the mountains, Dumont wanted him plagued by railway tracks blowing up on the prairies. He wanted to see Middleton turn back thousands of soldiers to walk for miles, skulking in fear because they did not know whether the animals or the Métis were the bigger threat. He told me later that he was thinking all this as he watched the posse members surrender their weapons to his men and put their hands behind their heads. I jumped down from my horse and strode over to him, hand outstretched.

—Today you changed my world, I said.

He shook my hand.

—If Riel had been like you, we could have changed the course of history for a people, he said.

—I feared you were tempted by a rout.

—I once raced headlong against a Blood on the prairie. When we were close enough to see the whites of each other's eyes, he turned. That was my success.

—I do not know how to thank you.

—You kept your promise. We have made a good trade.

The men of the posse sat on the road a long time, with their hands behind their heads. For the past two days they thought they were chasing down criminals. Instead, they stumbled into a war and found themselves on the wrong side. We collected twenty-five rifles, fifteen pistols, and enough ammunition to have extended the battle at Batoche for another week.

The governor told the assembly he was sorry to make them ride all this way because of his mistake. He pointed at the Pinkertons. Those men manufactured a criminal because they wanted one. They convinced a jury and then him of their lie. Because he now believed he had contributed to a travesty of justice, he was going to fix it.

The governor gestured for Wyatt to bring him the petition for pardon, which he placed on the haunch of his horse and signed. When he handed it back to Wyatt, Dumont gave the order to release the Younger brothers into his custody. The governor told the posse they were taking these men back as prisoners, and that Dumont had agreed to hand them over because he knew they were real lawbreakers. To show it was his will to return the Youngers, he handed the governor the only rifle his posse would now have to guard them on their ride back to the prison in Stillwater. No one asked why we took the Youngers in the first place.

Once the posse moved out, Dumont paid his men and released them from duty. It was good to see them pat each other's backs and celebrate their victory. Perhaps it was not the battle they most wanted to win. The sweetness of any victory, however, spilled over to ease past pain. It was not a day to quibble over whose injustice was overturned. They had righted a wrong.

Some men returned to Minnesota, Montana, and the Dakotas. Others accepted the amnesty and moved back to Saskatchewan. Wyatt and I joined Dumont on our long trek north to Lake Superior and back down many miles to Toronto, where Dumont left us and rode on alone to Québec. We had many nights of storytelling as we revisited our adventure.

With the donation I promised, Dumont continued on to Québec to continue fundraising before he eventually returned to his land at Batoche to live out the days he had left. He looked forward to evenings when he would sit and watch the sun slope down over the territory of his home, and think of the buffalo he and his men used to run. He pledged not to allow those thoughts to run to tragedy or hopelessness. He would have new thoughts.

Wyatt often talks about the ways the world has changed that we could never have predicted, and we are still relatively young. He was born at the beginning of the Civil War, when there was no telephone, no electric car, no refracting telescope, no vaccination for rabies, no time zones, and no cure for tuberculosis. There was no *Adventures of Huckleberry Finn* or a ticker-tape parade in New York. Who could have predicted that Billy the Kid would escape and then be shot and killed, or that PT Barnum's elephant, Jumbo, would behave like one of Wabigoon's moose and charge to its doom into an oncoming Grand Trunk train? My contribution to this reverie is to outline all that women can do now, with Susan B. Anthony voting (whether or not she was allowed to do so), Dr. Emily Stowe practising medicine here in Canada, and female attorneys arguing

Supreme Court cases in America. I still cannot believe that Geronimo surrendered. History marches along at the instigation of all kinds of decisions.

Now that our story is told, I will deposit this manuscript—along with the compass that Father gave to Mother and that I then gave to Wyatt, and the Pinkerton's and January's guns—in a safe deposit box in the bank at the end of our street. We bequeath all this to you, our daughter, Gabrielle, born in 1893, to discover upon our deaths. It will then be up to you how you want to understand your history. By the time you read this, you will have grown up in a bold new century for which your father and I hold much hope.

Today, July 6, 1897, you will see the Buffalo Bill Wild West Show in the large open-air arena at Dufferin and King Streets in Parkdale. There is no other use for this arena except to hold grand exhibitions.

Annie keeps Wyatt and me posted on the changes in Cody's show. The women riders have dispensed with sidesaddle and now ride like the men. Some even ride broncos. Their traditional roles in the show as prairie Madonnas or Indian captives are still the same, but the total number of women employed by Cody has fallen. At least, Annie reports, the women are paid the same rates as the men. These days, there appears to be more interest in seeing military displays alongside the cowboys. Perhaps now that America has military adventures in other parts of the world, people want to see their exploits exhibited at home. I am sure there will come a day when Cody's show will cease to draw crowds. For now, the North American imagination is as swept up with the promise of freedom and the open range as it was when I was in the show.

According to the newspaper, there will be a parade through Toronto's downtown city streets and then two performances featuring great displays of horsemanship and shooting ability. There will be special appearances of the cavalry, an Arab troupe of athletes performing a clever pyramid, and, of course, the Deadwood Stage pursued by Indians determined to keep the white man from taking over their land. After the two-hour show, we will put you to bed, dear Gabrielle, and Annie and Frank will join us for a late-night dinner. We will toast Gabriel Dumont and share a few laughs about old times.

ACKNOWLEDGEMENTS

I would like to thank the Ontario Arts Council for its support, and specifically Laurence Steven for his early encouragement.

I have benefitted from the research of many, but would like to mention three books that were particularly helpful: *Gabriel Dumont Speaks* translated by Michael Barnholden; *Riel and the Rebellion 1885 Reconsidered* by Thomas Flanagan; and *The Life and Legacy of Annie Oakley* by Glenda Riley.

Preparing a novel for publication involves good judgment and many sets of eyes. Thank you to editor Melva McLean for her helpful insights about structure. Much thanks to my publisher, Taryn Boyd, for her superlative taste in fiction and for supporting my vision with such consistent enthusiasm.

Finally, to my stalwart wingmen: Gannon, who helped with grand insights right down to picky details, and Gary, who has faithfully read every word I have put on paper. You both really must love me.

CINDA GAULT holds a PhD in English, with a specialty in Canadian national identity issues in women's writing of the 1960s and 1970s. She teaches and writes about Canadian literature, and lives in Toronto, Ontario. Visit her at www.cindagault.com.